DEFENDER

NIGHT WAR SAGA: BOOK TWO

by
S.T. Bende and Leia Stone

DEDICATION

For all of Midgard's defenders—never stop
fighting on.

CHAPTER ONE

"PEPPER, YOU'RE KILLING ME here." Tore stood in front of the open oven. He fanned black smoke toward the open window while Mack disabled the smoke alarm.

Frustration simmered behind my furrowed brow. "Sorry. I wanted to surprise you guys. I read the instructions. I don't understand what went wrong."

When the bulk of the black cloud had exited the kitchen, Tore shook his head. He pulled my charred lasagna out of the oven and placed it on the counter. Stepping closer to me, he turned to tuck a stray piece of blonde hair behind my ear. "Look, you've got brains, beauty, and this week, I taught you how to kill a man with your bare hands. You don't have to add master chef to that list, okay?" He kissed my forehead, and my frustration gave way to warm waves of gratitude.

Dear Universe, Thanks for sending me a boyfriend who likes me just the way I am—nonexistent cooking skills and all. Xoxo, Allie.

"Master chef?" Johann snorted. "I think she was aiming for mediocre pre-made-dinner maker."

My neck grew warm, and to mask my embarrassment, I spun around and socked Johann in the arm. He shot me a cheeky wink, clearly enjoying another opportunity to give me a hard time.

Oh, you'll get yours, Johann. Just you wait.

"How do you burn a frozen lasagna?" Bodie studied the instructions on the empty carton.

Mack sighed. "If Allie placed the dish into the oven before the temperature reached four hundred degrees, the rise in—"

"All right. I get it." The heat crept from my neck up to my cheeks. I threw my hands in the air, hoping to put a stop to the analysis of my culinary shortcomings. "The kitchen is off limits. I'll leave the cooking to the experts. Now, someone order pizza because I'm starving."

"You and me both," Johann agreed. Mack dialed the pizza place while Bodie helped me discard the remains of my epic lasagna fail. It would be takeout for dinner then. But at least it wouldn't be baked chicken breasts again. Thank God.

Three weeks had passed since I'd nearly died on the side of a mountain in Jotunheim, where my protectors and I had traveled to retrieve a piece of my immortal weapon, Gud Morder. After a harrowing encounter with a frost giant and an influx of dark energy that left me all but wishing for my death, I'd woken up in the Asgardian healing unit. There, I found the protector who'd owned my heart since the first time I'd pepper sprayed him, sitting vigil at my bedside. Tore had ensured I received the best care Asgard's healing team could provide. But once I'd been cleared for release, Tore and the boys had lit into me with a training regimen designed to ensure I'd never be caught unprepared on a dark realm again. After all, the remaining six pieces of Gud Morder had to be found before we could kill the evil night goddess, Nott, and wake my mother from her cursed Night Sleep.

The guys had been relentlessly drilling me in hand-to-hand combat, teaching me to use the arsenal of weapons contained in the complex, and stuffing me with more protein-packed meals than I could have imagined possible. My protectors were still determined to up my muscle mass, despite my finally being able to pin Johann in a fight. I'd gotten a verbal agreement from Mack that when I could pin him, he'd cook me homemade pizza whenever I wanted. And so, my insane training regimen continued.

Apparently, the slogan around here was No Rest for the Demigod. Ever.

"Any news on your mom today, Allie?" Bodie asked. "Those dark energy cords in her centers were some scary skit."

"No kidding." I shuddered, remembering the black swirls that had threatened to suck the life from my mother's body. Greta and I were lucky we'd gotten to her in time to remove them—and we were even luckier that they hadn't found a way to come back.

"She still doing okay?" Bodie asked.

"She is." Relief pinged through me as I relayed news of my mom's continued improvement. "Greta says there still haven't been any residual effects from the energy drains, and her vitals are actually up from what they were a few days ago. She's sleeping more peacefully now."

"I'm glad to hear it." Bodie wiped his hands on a dishtowel.

So was I. My mom's stability gave me the hope I needed to push forward, despite the fact that a dark goddess and her legion of night elf minions were gunning for my soul and trying to end the world as we knew it. Add in the fact that Tore was now referring to me as his girlfriend, and demigod life was slowly looking up.

Even if I was an abysmal failure in the kitchen.

"Pizza will be here in half an hour." Mack tucked his phone in his pocket before wiping a few charred bits from the counter to the sink. "And Greta will be here sooner than that, so it's time to tidy up." He turned on one combat-booted heel and marched toward the living room.

"Wait. What? Did you know Greta was coming over?" Bodie hissed at Johann.

"Nope." Johann shrugged. "But Mack could have mentioned it. I don't pay attention to most of what he says."

"I heard that," Mack called from the other room. "And unless these socks are going to fold themselves, I suggest you take your laundry into your room."

"I was going to," Johann huffed.

"Don't make me tell your fathers they raised a slob." I could practically hear Mack's head shake.

I snorted.

"You too, missy." Mack reappeared in the kitchen doorway. "There's a pile of books in front of the fireplace, and I'm pretty sure the four of us haven't read Dark Elf Combat For Dummies since primary school."

"On it." I dusted the last of the blackened lasagna guts from my hands. As I turned away from the sink, Tore's warm hand wrapped possessively around my wrist. Oh, yum. He spun me into his chest, snaked his arms low around my back, and gave my butt a firm squeeze. Lowering his lips to mine, he claimed my mouth in a deliciously languid kiss. Blood left my brain on a southbound expressway, igniting a searing heat somewhere just south of my navel. My fingertips wove through Tore's long, blond hair, and I pulled his face closer to mine, all the while pressing my torso against his.

Bodie's irritated groan interrupted us. "Come on. Again?"

"Go away, Bodie," Tore growled. His chest rumbled against mine as he spoke.

"Bodie, perhaps you might want to focus your attention on cleaning the downstairs bathroom," Mack suggested. "Unless you want Greta to think she's visiting a pack of wild animals. Honestly, would it kill you to trim your facial hair in your own bathroom?"

"The lighting's better downstairs." Bodie rubbed the stubble that lined his jaw. His cocoa-colored skin was dotted pink at the cheeks and ears.

As Bodie grabbed his phone off the counter and backed out of the kitchen, I lowered my voice so that only Tore could hear. "What's with Bodie and Greta? Any history there?"

Tore's mouth quirked into a lopsided grin. "Bodie's been in love with Greta since we were kids. He tried to kiss her at a party, and it didn't go well."

"Ha. Didn't go well?" Bodie's voice came from the hallway. I cringed as I spun around to see him re-entering the kitchen. So much for whispering. "I leaned in and tripped. My teeth crashed into Greta's mouth so hard that she bled for half an hour."

I winced. That sounded pretty awful. But instead of offering sympathy, Tore tried to hide a grin.

"Why are you smiling, Vidarsson? I built that woman up in my head for years. Finally got my chance and I blew it. I mean, she needed stiches. It was terrible."

Tore laughed. "It was awful at the time, but it's funny now. You should still go for it."

Mack strode through the kitchen doorway with a bottle of cleaning wipes in one hand. "Love is a fickle thing, my friend. But true rewards come to those who persevere in the face of adversity." He tilted his head at the wipes.

Bodie snatched them up with a groan. "Thanks, fortune cookie. Now, if you'll excuse me, I've got a bathroom to clean."

Mack turned his gaze on me. "Allie, your books."

"Right. Sorry." With tremendous effort, I tried to extract myself from Tore's embrace. He just held on tighter, pulling me in for another kiss. My heart thudded as he ran his tongue along my bottom lip. I finally broke away with a breathless, "Hold that thought," before ducking out of the kitchen.

"Seriously, Pepper," Tore called to my retreating back. "Killing me!"

"Blame Mack!" I shouted back.

I entered the living room to find Johann hurriedly shoving clean laundry into a basket. With a smile, I picked up my books and carried them to my room. My nightstand was already filled with protector-required reading, so I set the texts on the ground beside my bed before popping my head back into the hall. "Hey, Mack?" I shouted.

"Yes?" The light elf glided calmly down the hallway.

"Do we need to clean up the den for Greta?" I asked.

"Good point. Johann, you'll need to fetch the rest of your clean clothes from the den so Greta has a place to sleep." Mack smiled serenely.

"I'm going there!" Johann huffed again. "I swear, living with you is worse than living with my dads."

"They did you no favors by doing your laundry until you moved out." Mack shrugged. "You'll thank me some day."

A flash of light from outside drew my attention to my bedroom window. The white sheers that covered the glass filled with a kaleidoscope of color, morphing from red to orange, all the way down the spectrum to indigo. Happiness bubbled in my fourth energy center as my heart filled with warmth. "Greta's here!"

"Already?" Bodie's panicked voice rang out. A glance down the hallway toward the bathroom revealed the six-foot-plus Asgardian still frantically scrubbing the sink.

"Need help?" Tore sauntered out of the kitchen.

"Nope. I'm good." Bodie threw his cleaning wipe in the garbage, tossed the container beneath the sink, and turned on the tap. He scrubbed off the scent of bleach, then turned the water off and stepped into the hallway. "All done."

"Your hands." Tore pointed to the dripping digits.

"Oh. Right." Bodie wiped his hands on his pants and leaned casually against the wall.

"Dude." Johann laughed. His spiky, black hair was a blur as he charged up the stairs with his overflowing laundry basket. "Try to act cooler once Greta's inside, okay?"

"Shut up," Bodie muttered.

"Seriously?" Tore raised one dark blond eyebrow. "No 'that's what she said?' Come on, man, he set you up."

"I said shut up." Bodie's ears re-pinked into an adorable shade of embarrassment.

A light rap on the door set Bodie's shoulders back. He drew himself up to his full height and stalked toward the door. "I'll get it."

Mack and I cleared out of his way, moving to stand at the end of the hallway beside Tore. My favorite protector held out his arms, and I nestled in, fighting back a goofy grin from the warm fuzzies that spread through me when he placed a possessive hand over my abdomen. Mine, it seemed to say. And I was only too happy to be claimed. My near-death experience had knocked a bit of the jerk out of him, and while he still had his issues, and more often than not irritated the hell out of me with his closed-off energy, my gut told me we'd smooth out our rough spots together. We were demigods; we had plenty of time.

"Hey, Greta." Bodie cracked the door open. His energy radiated a sunshiny yellow, the joy evident in every fiber of his being. So cute.

"Hei hei, Bodie." Greta's tinkling voice came from the porch. "Well? Are you going to let me in?"

"Oh, right. Sorry." Bodie threw the door the rest of the way open, and our petite healer friend stepped into the hall. "Here, let me take your bag. Mack's setting you up in the den. That okay?"

"It's perfekt. Takk." Greta handed Bodie her overnight bag but held on to her healing kit. While Bodie carried her gear to her room, Greta tossed her strawberry braid over her shoulder and dusted white powder from its strands.

"Velkommen, Greta. Is it still snowing out there?" Mack asked.

"Ja. Hei, guys." Greta's eyes darted to Tore's arm around me, then back up to my face with a wink. "Can't wait to get started on our energy training, Allie."

"You and me both." I still needed all the help I could get.

"Hei, Greta." Johann jogged down the stairs and pinned Mack with a glare. "There. House up to your standards?"

"It will do." Mack nodded.

I tried not to laugh out loud at the brotherly dynamic between my protectors. I didn't have much by way of family of origin. My dad, an Asgardian warrior, had died before I was born, and my kick-butt warrior granny had been killed a few months ago while protecting me from a dark entity. And my mom, well, until my protectors came into my life and told me otherwise, I'd thought she was dead, too. But the family I now chose to be a part of was every bit as important to me as the family I'd been born into.

Even when said family bickered over laundry like ornery old men.

Mack crossed to the front door and lifted a set of keys from the hook. "Johann, would you care to go with me to pick up the pizza?"

"Only if you promise not to lecture me on the proper way to fold underwear." Johann pulled two jackets out of the coat closet and tossed one at Mack. Bodie chuckled as he exited the den.

"I thought you ordered delivery?" I questioned.

"You don't think Mack gave the pizza place our real address, do you?" Johann shook his head. "Rule number one of the safe house, Allie. Don't tell delivery guys the location of the safe house."

Right.

"See you in a few," Mack said as he and Johann stepped onto the porch.

"Bye." I waggled my fingers. When the door clicked closed behind them, I slid my hand over Tore's and twined my fingers through his. "Come on, Protector. Let's ask Greta what's been happening in Asgard."

"Or we could leave Bodie to embarrass himself in front of Greta, and you and I could head upstairs for some alone time." Tore shot me my favorite dimpled grin.

"I wish." I really did. Alone time was in short supply. All of my protectors—including Tore—were one hundred percent focused on getting me battle ready. They'd gone so far as to pin their insanely intense schedule to the refrigerator. Between sleeping, eating, and training, there was no time left over for what I really wanted to be doing.

"I mean it." Tore winked. "Mack said we had a few minutes."

"I think we're going to need more than a few minutes." I gave him a pointed look, and his eyes flared like two cobalt firepits. With a low growl, he ran his gaze up and down my body. The look sent another pulse due south. Good God, he was hot. We hadn't gone all the way yet, and while I understood we had priorities, I couldn't help but wish we had more time for ourselves. Not only was Tore ridiculously good-looking, but he'd saved my life—twice—and he was literally a demigod. I knew killing Nott was important, but couldn't a girl multitask? I mean, seriously?

My overworked heart breathed a tiny sigh of relief when the flame in Tore's eyes died down to the normal sea blue hue. "Fair enough." He bent down to brush his lips against my ear, sending an icy shiver racing down my spine. Holy hot demigod. "But one day soon, when all of this Nott skit is behind us, I'm taking you away from all these guys. Somewhere warm." He raked his teeth along my earlobe, and the shiver shot back up with a vengeance. "Clothing optional."

The thought of Tore without clothing turned my brain to mush. I was totally done for.

"So, tell us, Greta." Tore tugged at my hand, leading me and my inferno-laced cheeks into the living room. "What's new in Asgard?"

"It's been fairly quiet. Eir's still in the healing unit, more for her own safety than anything else at this point. The Alfödr has two warriors stationed outside her door and one on the roof of the structure. I check in on her twice a day, and she's remaining stable." Greta sat on the loveseat beside the fireplace, leaving a disappointed-looking Bodie to join Tore and me on the L-shaped sectional.

"Has the Alfödr said any more about Nott? Any leads on the weapon?" Bodie leaned forward.

"None." Greta shook her head. Another flurry of snow fell from her braid and landed on her lap.

"It must be coming down pretty hard out there." I glanced out the window. Sure enough, fat, white clumps fell against the backdrop of thick evergreens. "Jeez, this blizzard's been going on for days. We were lucky it broke long enough for Heimdall to drop in Greta's Bifrost, but it picked up again in a hurry. This weather pattern has to let up soon."

"Does it?" Tore slid his arm around my shoulders and pulled me to his side. "Nott's been wreaking havoc on Midgard for years, and the mortals weren't doing much to offset the effects of climate change. It was bound to catch up eventually."

"I guess." I sighed. "So, no word on the weapon pieces? Dang it. I guess we'll just have to wait for—" A fierce pounding on the front door made me lose focus. "Who's that?"

"Open up!" Johann's shout was followed by heavy steps. A second later, a key clicked in the lock, and the door flew open. Johann and Mack stumbled inside, bringing with them countless snowflakes, four pizzas, and one dead raven.

"Holy Hel." Tore jumped to his feet, nearly face-planting me into the coffee table. "Is that—"

"Huginn," Mack confirmed. "We ran a perimeter check on our way back and found him just outside the barrier."

"Oh my gods, is he okay?" Greta dropped to her knees in front of the coffee table and gestured for Mack to lay the Alfödr's messenger-raven down. My light elf friend carried the bird into the living room and set him on Greta's makeshift veterinary table. Mack was so distraught, he didn't even notice all the snow he'd tracked over his pristine wood floor.

"Why couldn't Huginn penetrate the barrier?" Tore barked. "We set the shield around the safe house to allow Huginn, Muninn, and direct Bifrost transports in. It blocks all other non-resident entrants, but the bird should have made it through. We haven't changed the frequency."

"No idea." Johann set the pizzas on an end table before kneeling beside Greta. He pulled a tiny scroll from his pocket and held it up. "But we found this a few yards away from him. There's a thread around his foot; it looks like he was carrying it."

Tore snatched the scroll from his hands. His eyes moved back and forth as he scanned its contents.

"What's it say?" I peered over his shoulder.

"One of the Alfödr's contacts in Nidavellir spotted some dark entities atop one of their mountains," Tore summarized.

"Not another mountain," I groaned. "I barely made it off the last one."

"We can worry about the tip later." Bodie leaned over the table. "Greta, can you save Huginn?"

"Ja, I do not want to be the one to tell the Alfödr our protective barrier killed his bird." Johann shuddered.

"Nothing killed him yet. He's just in shock." Greta held her hands over the creature. I reached out with my own energy and sensed a flicker of light from behind Huginn's ribs. Thank the maker. I didn't want to tell the head of Asgard we'd offed his pet, either. Odin the Alfödr was a scary-intense ruler who wore an eyepatch. That accessory alone upped his intimidation factor a billion percent.

"What shocked Huginn? Was it our shield?" Mack asked.

"No. I think . . . ah. There it is." Greta placed her fingers on the bird's chest and withdrew a small dart. "He was shot."

"That close to the barrier?" Johann's eyes widened. "We found him a few yards from our border. Nobody knows where we are . . . do they?"

"Not sure, but we'd better extend the protections. And possibly set a new shield." Mack's eyes rolled skyward in the inter-realm expression of mental math. He was probably recalculating how to extend whatever magical cloak protected our little compound.

"Greta," Bodie said through gritted teeth, "Can you save Huginn?"

"Yes. It's not a dark magic malady; it seems like a Midgardian tranquilizer." Greta sighed. "It's possible this just came from some kids playing too far out in the woods. But I'd increase the protections, just in case."

"On it." Mack nodded.

"Now, everybody quiet. I need to focus. Allie, you want to help me out?" Greta reached into her healing bag and withdrew a crystal wand.

"Uh, sure. What do you want me to do?"

"Call up the Liv. I'll infuse Huginn with crystal energy where I have extracted the dart. If you give him a dose of your healing power, we'll send him back to the Alfödr in tip-top shape." Greta placed one hand atop the bird's chest.

"Should I get my armor?" I asked.

"I think you're ready to channel the Liv without it. Your necklace should be able to harness any overflow at this point." Greta used her wand to tap the white gem that hung from my neck. It emitted a pulse of light at the contact.

Don't freak out. Don't freak out. The Liv won't accidentally kill you . . . I hope.

"Okay." I pushed down my panic and positioned myself closer to Greta. With a breath, I called up the life-giving energy that lived beneath my ribcage. It pooled in my chest, drawing into my necklace and holding a steady pulse that resonated from my heart to the gem and back again. "Liv's ready," I confirmed.

"Great." Greta laid her wand beside Huginn and placed her fingertips atop his chest. He was still—too still. Greta lightly massaged the place where she had extracted the dart moments ago and picked up her wand. "Allie, send a shot of the Liv into the wound, and I'll seal it up."

"All right." I placed my left hand over Huginn and drew the Liv into my shoulder. It traveled down my arm, through my palm, and sent a glowing blue beam at the bird. His chest rose in one jerky movement. I pulled my hand back while Greta waved her wand in a figure-eight pattern over the raven. His body shuddered with one deep breath. A second followed, then a third. And we all exhaled in relief.

"Oh, thank gods," Mack said.

I let the Liv simmer out of my system. It hadn't killed me without my armor. For this, I was grateful.

Tore reached over to squeeze my hand. "We need to get him back to the Alfödr. Like Greta said, it was probably just some kid who wandered too far into the woods. But in case it wasn't, Odin will want to have him looked after."

"I'll take him back," I volunteered. It had been three weeks since I'd seen my mom. It would be nice to spend time with her.

"No can do." Tore's long, blond hair moved against his shoulders. "Huginn brought us a tip, and we need to follow it up by going to Nidavellir. But the dwarves can be nasty buggers. If we're going to their realm, Greta's going to need to teach you how to harness your energy for defense."

"The Liv?" I paused. "I thought it was supposed to create life—not destroy it."

"It can do both. Greta will explain." Tore looked around the table, where Mack, Johann, and Bodie all hovered over the now-breathing bird. "Pizza's going to get cold, so everybody eat up. Then Mack, you need to stay here and enhance the compound's protections with me while Greta works with Allie. Bodie, you and Johann take Huginn home to Asgard. Spend the night with Bodie's parents if you want to, or pop over to Vanaheim and say hei to Johann's family. Just be back here by sunrise tomorrow."

"What happens at sunrise?" I asked, hoping desperately the answer was Mack makes us a mouthwatering brunch. Or even better, Allie and I go on a super special date.

Tore eyed me levelly, no hint of brunch or dates in his icy blue gaze. "Tomorrow at sunrise, we pay the dwarves a little visit. We're going to bring another piece of Gud Morder home."

CHAPTER TWO

AFTER THE BOYS TOOK off with Huginn, Greta and I set to work on 'energy warfare training.' Because that was a thing now. Why I couldn't just wave some crystal wands around like Greta, I did not know.

My friend had devoted the past few weeks to teaching me to single-handedly create shields. Mack's team of doppelganger brothers—who I affectionately referred to as the Mack Pack—had used their swords to create a shield that had protected me from a night elf attack in Alfheim. And Greta had insisted on making sure I knew how to form one on my own. Now, it was time to learn offensive tactics—Greta was going to teach me to make a weapon from the Liv. The energetic power to give life had transferred itself to me while my mother was trapped in the Night Sleep. And since I was its keeper, I was tasked with yielding it, not only for protection, but apparently, for attack. *No pressure.*

The corners of my mouth tugged downward as Greta set up a perimeter of crystals around the living room. "If the Liv is supposed to heal people, why are we using it as a weapon?"

Greta completed her circle by placing the final crystal in front of the fireplace, then spun around to face me. Her green eyes blazed when she spoke. "Healers are warriors against the darkness. If we don't fight with all the light we have, the realms will plunge into chaos. You've seen that firsthand."

Her words sent flashes of memories across my mind—the black swirl rising over my mother, the treatises on deforestation and the ensuing species depletion I'd read in Environmental Studies, the reports of the torrential downpours in Los Angeles and the subsequent mudslides that destroyed homes and killed hikers. Despite the humans' lack of awareness, the fact of the matter was that we were all in the midst of war. A war not only for my mother's life, but for the future of Midgard, and for the power of light in all the realms. Greta was right—if we didn't utilize every tool in our arsenal, we'd fail to protect the realms from Nott's destruction.

Which meant we had to be prepared to use the power of life to kill.

I drew my shoulders back with resolve. "You're sure I can do this?"

Greta raised one perfectly-groomed brow. "Your mother once took the heads off three dark elves with one snap of her light whip. I have no doubt that you can do the same."

My mouth popped open. "Light whip?"

"Fun, right?" Greta grinned. "We should probably be practicing this in the complex, but it's too cold to go outside. So, try not to burn the house down, okay?"

My newfound confidence took a nosedive. Was she serious? Could I actually destroy the cabin? *Note to self: If I ever become an energy teacher, don't tell students not to burn the house down before a lesson.*

Greta walked over to her healing bag and removed two crystal wands. She waved them back and forth across her body before returning her attention to me. "The crystals along the perimeter of the room will help intensify the charge of your whip, make it easier to summon while you're still learning. I'm going to help you the first time, but then I want you to do it yourself. Deal?"

My stomach balled in a knot of nerves, but I nodded. So much for my impression of the Liv as a friendly, life-affirming entity. Now that I knew it could hurt someone, calling it up seemed a whole lot riskier.

Greta correctly interpreted my furrowed brow. She reassured me with a gentle hand pat. "Don't worry, Allie. I'm not a dark entity. The Liv won't hurt me."

Whew. Potential crisis averted. I released the breath I'd been holding. "The Liv can only hurt dark beings? You should have started with that."

Greta laughed. "Relax. The worst it can do is knock me out for a few minutes."

"What? I don't want to knock you out!" Frustration coursed through me, and I tossed my hands in the air. "Greta, I think I'm in over my head. Maybe we should just go back to forming the shield, and I'll try to bring whoever I need to protect inside it with me."

"That's not always going to be enough." Greta eyed me levelly. "Tore, Mack, Johann, and Bodie are your protectors, but what if someone gets through all of them?"

"Then I fight with my sword," I suggested.

"Swords will work on a night elf," Greta agreed. "But on the darker beings, on Nott . . . you need to learn to turn the Liv into a weapon. Come on." She positioned herself in front of me and raised her crystal wands as if they were swords. "Call forth the Liv."

"Right." I took a deep breath, shaking off my anxiety. Then I felt for the pulse, the living energy that crackled just below the surface of my torso. When the Liv flickered to life, I latched onto it. I drew it up through my ribs, ran it across my shoulders, and let it drain down my arm. The blue light flared out of my palm, and Greta narrowed her eyes.

"*Veldig bra.* Very good," she translated. *Veldig bra?* I seriously needed to take some Norwegian lessons. And some Swedish lessons. The guys had told me they spoke a mashup of the two languages—a hybrid they referred to as 'Scandiwegian.' Clearly, I needed to study *that* if I wanted to keep up.

Greta moved back and forth in front of the blue ball that pulsed in my palm, working her crystal wands in and out. The elongated stones shaped the Liv into a thin stream of light. It stretched a full six feet in length, growing thinner and tapering into a wisp at its end.

Holy Lord. I stood staring at the long, blue weapon with a crooked grin. "You made a whip. That is seriously epic."

"Focus, Allie," Greta admonished. "It's losing its shape."

Sure enough, the whip had fallen flat. It now stretched across the length of the living room like a soggy noodle. *Oops.* The Liv reminded me of its power by poking me repeatedly from inside my chest. Each poke served as a reminder that the Liv was supposed to be the energetic manifestation of life, not a magic noodle of limpness.

Sorry, Liv.

I fortified the surge through my palms, refocusing on the weapon until it took shape again. When the blue glow stiffened to re-form a thick rope, Greta shifted. She took several steps away from me, so her shoulder was pressed against the fireplace. "Better. Okay, now try to crack it."

My eyes widened. "I've never used a whip before. I have no idea how to do that."

"Fair enough. You're going to want to do this." Greta raised her arm over her head and quickly pulled it to her waist. "Physical whips are cumbersome. Their weight and length make it difficult for an average-sized mortal to generate the velocity needed to elicit a crack. But you're not a mortal, and this isn't a physical whip. It's energetic. Draw on your demigod strength, and you'll easily control it."

Because *that* made sense. *Not.*

"Show me?" I asked.

Greta nodded. "You're right-handed, correct?"

"Yup."

"Okay. Then follow me." Greta slowly raised her right arm, held for a beat, then lowered it. I did the same; the whip fluttered with the gentle movement.

"Nothing happened," I muttered.

"Well of course not." Greta tossed her strawberry braid over her shoulder. "That was quarter speed. Do it again with me." She repeated the movement, this time bringing her arm up, holding, and snapping it down at a slightly faster pace. When I imitated her, the whip fluttered with more intensity. It sent a jolt back through my palm as if it was irritated with me.

"I think the Liv wants to go faster," I guessed.

"Then let's give it what it wants." The corners of Greta's lips pulled back in a grin.

With a nod, I tightened my hand around the light whip. *Fine, Liv. But you're answering to Mack if you burn the house down.*

Greta raised her arm, paused, and snapped it down so fast that the motion was a blur. I took a grounding breath and did the same, holding my hand above my head until the coils of energy threatened to unfurl. I snapped my arm down, yelping at the loud burst of noise that erupted though the living room. The blue pulse of light detonated just below the high beams of the ceiling.

Crap. I squeezed my eyes shut, trying to remember where the guys kept the fire extinguishers.

"Yes!" Greta shouted. "You did it!"

I opened one eye, then exhaled in relief. The house was fire-free. And I'd actually managed to crack my first energy whip without hurting my friend. *Thank God.*

"That was the hottest thing I've ever seen."

I jumped at the sound of Tore's gruff voice. My focus ebbed, and my whip went back into limp noodle mode before slowly fizzling out. *Oops.* I turned my head toward the doorway and gave my favorite protector a wink as Greta charged at him, waving her hands as if he were a household pest.

"Get out of here. You're distracting my student," Greta admonished.

Tore's gaze moved up and down my body, lingering on my chest for a second longer than necessary. My temperature rose at his appreciative stare. *Yum.* "You're bringing that whip on the vacation we talked about," he ordered.

My brain ran through a thousand scenarios, each more blush-worthy than the last. When I finally managed to squeak out a weak "okay," Tore had already turned on one heel and marched down the hallway. His black cargos hugged the muscles of his butt with each step. The boy deserved a trophy for that butt.

My resolve to learn *all the things* strengthened tenfold. We were going to defeat Nott super-fast, or I was going to lose my mind. I *really* needed to take that vacation.

Greta sighed wistfully. "Young love."

"What about you?" I hurriedly changed the subject. "Dating anyone?"

I wasn't just deflecting; I genuinely wanted to know if she was interested in Bodie. Maybe the whole bloody kiss incident wasn't the big deal he thought it was.

Greta knelt down to rifle through her backpack. "I don't have time to date. We're way understaffed in Asgard. Maybe I'll be able to think about guys when the realm gets a few more healers."

Hmm. A quick scan of Greta's energy revealed a brown blob over her heart. It flickered for the briefest moment but disappeared before I could follow its trail to the source. Dark spots in the fourth center usually indicated an emotional injury, and I wanted to ask my friend if everything was okay. But Greta continued rifling through healing supplies without offering up any additional information. It seemed pretty clear she didn't want to talk about her dating life—and it wasn't my place to outright ask who had hurt her heart. I'd just have to hope she'd open up to me in time.

"What the . . . oh, Hel." Greta jumped backward, dropping her backpack onto the ground. With a loud clatter, a large, glass jar rolled out of Greta's sack and onto the wood floor. A furry, brown creature flopped around inside. It shimmered with a sticky energy unlike anything I'd seen before. The creature raised its head slowly, as if it was just coming into consciousness. When it opened the lids of its beady, crimson eyes, I was hit with a wave of darkness. My stomach churned as nausea rolled through me. *Yikes.* Whatever this creature was, it was bigtime bad news.

"Did you bring that thing here?" I balked.

"Not knowingly." Greta's eyes widened. "I'd have sensed that energy a mile away. It must have been *severely* sedated—almost to the point of death."

At Greta's last word, the creature clawed its way out of the jar and scurried toward the couch. It had most definitely left death's door.

"What is that thing?" I backed up so my shoulder blades were pressed against the fireplace.

"Don't move, Allie." Greta scooped up her bag and shoved her hand inside. She withdrew a handful of crystals and flung them at each corner of the living room. Now the earlier perimeter was inlaid with clusters of thick, white stones.

"Wasn't planning on it," I muttered. "Unless that thing comes back out from under the—oh my God!"

The creature darted across the living room, gunning it for the hallway. When it reached the crystals, it jumped backward as if it had been shocked.

"Good. The protection's holding. Careful, Allie. That creature is extremely dangerous."

"What the hell is it?" I asked again.

"It's a fire-breathing rat from Muspelheim. We found a portal not far from the healing unit, and before we could seal it off, a few of these little monsters snuck through. I thought the warriors destroyed them all, though. I have no idea how one got into my bag." Greta shuddered. I didn't blame her. A hitchhiking fire-breather was about the worst surprise I could imagine.

"Why didn't you notice it was in your bag when you were removing the crystals in the first—oh my God, it's moving again!" My butt slammed into the corner of the couch as I leapt from the path of the red-eyed rodent. Its pointy, yellow fangs snapped angrily as it circled the living room.

"It was inside the energy containment vessel—the jar I use to trap dark energy that I pull from patients. It was empty when I packed it . . ." Greta sidestepped the creature with considerably more calm than I felt. Her eyes narrowed. "Someone must have placed the rat in there."

Oh, come *on.* Couldn't a girl catch a break? "Who would do that?"

Greta ran her bottom lip between her teeth. "Someone who knew I was coming here . . . who knew I'd have access to the safe house. Allie, this is not good."

Well, no *skit.*

Without warning, the rat raised its scraggly head to reveal two tendrils of smoke streaming from its nose.

"How do we get rid of it?" I blurted.

"Get that light whip running, Allie. You're going to have to kill it."

Crazy Asgardian healer said what? "I don't know if I can—"

"Do you want to have to explain to Mack why his imported rug got singed by a fire-breather? Or worse, why his entire living room went up in flames?" Greta stared at the now-snarling animal.

Of course I didn't. I wasn't sure what scared me more—a fire-breathing rodent or the wrath of Midgard's tidiest protector. I wrapped my arms around my chest and held tight. This exercise was *not* what I'd had in mind when Greta popped in for our lesson.

Though in all fairness, Greta seemed equally surprised at the recent turn of events. Stupid, hitchhiking rat.

"You ready?" Greta raised one perfectly-shaped brow.

"I . . . uh . . ." I hemmed.

"Think fast, Allie. One of these burned down an entire village in Alfhiem last year. They're awful little monsters—they're crawling with dark energy, and they're only too happy to infect you with it. Don't feel bad about killing this one."

At the mention of dark energy, icicles wove through my vertebrae. I willed them back down with an audible gulp. This was *not* the time to reminisce about the hell I'd experienced in Jotunheim.

"Wait." I paused. "There was a rat in Alfheim? I thought you said they were from Muspelheim. How'd one get onto Mack's realm?"

"Don't know." Greta shrugged. "The fire giants could have sent one through a portal. Or maybe one snuck back with one of the light elf warriors when he returned from a training mission."

The thought of this creature hurting Mack's family—my god family—and their beautiful village set me on edge. I was on board with killing the tiny beast.

"All right. I'll try." I drew a breath and called forth the Liv. Energy surged from my chest, filled my shoulder, and cascaded down my arm like a beautiful, blue waterfall. The power pooled in my hand but refused to mold into the weapon I needed it to be. My eyes met Greta's in a hopeful look. "Can you help me?"

"Sorry." Greta shook her head. "You have to learn to do it yourself."

A frustrated grunt escaped my lips as the sharp-fanged rodent let out a low hiss. I was all for tough love when the situation warranted it, but this was taking it too far. Even Socrates would have abandoned his teaching method if his students were faced with fire-breathing rats. Then again, Socrates wouldn't have made his students kill demon rodents, period. Greta had some *serious* issues.

"Tick tock, Allie. It's going to start snorting flames."

Crap.

I focused my energy on the Liv—my only defense against the flame-breather clawing at the ground. My hands moved deftly up and down as I molded my weapon. The sound of air hissing through teeth and claws scuttling against the hardwood floor drew my attention back to the rat. It was on the move again, running frantically across the living room. When it slammed against the crystal border, it shrank backward with a snarl.

"Focus!" Greta called out. I studied my hands, only to discover the Liv was still more 'wet noodle' than 'fierce light whip.' *Dang it.*

"You haven't been doing your meditations," Greta scolded.

She was right. My days at the safe house were so over-scheduled that I didn't have time to meditate until the very end of the day. And since Tore walked me to my room every night, and said walks tended to result in pretty intense make-out sessions—sessions that lasted until Mack charged down the stairs and demanded we break it up so I'd be rested for morning training . . . well, meditation had taken a backseat to the study of Tore's lips.

I had zero regrets about my choice.

"The rat's going to breathe fire on Mack's area rug if you don't pull it together," Greta sing-songed.

Crappers. I snapped back to attention, releasing my thoughts of Tore's masterful lips and focusing really hard on the Liv. The energy was an extension of me, of every living thing that was good in the realms. It had chosen *me* to manifest itself in, at least until it could return to my mother, and I would not let it down. With my resolve, the limp noodle stiffened in my grasp. The fine rope of the light whip formed, sparking to life with an energetic jolt. I grinned. *One crispy rat, coming right up.*

"The rat's breath is smoking," Greta warned. "Mack's not going to be happy if you don't do something to save his rug. Step it up, Allie."

I focused my gaze on the spot where the rat stamped its little feet. The creature was backed against the couch, its scraggly-haired head turning from Greta's crystal wands to my blue whip and back again. It must have determined I was the lesser threat, because it lowered its head and charged at me. With a sharp flick of my wrist, my weapon emitted a loud *crack*. At the sound, the rat turned one hundred and eighty degrees and scurried back toward the couch. A steady stream of fire flowed from its mouth as it ran. *Yikes.* The trail wasn't very long, but it was low to the ground, and packed a powerful heat. I cringed at the singed black balls now resting atop the area rug. Mack was going to kill me. Ratty needed to die, like yesterday. I raised and lowered my arm, then snapped it back up with a fierce movement. The rodent was a step ahead of me, scuttling out of the way just before my whip cracked. The blue light lashed against the carpet, and for a second, I feared Mack would have a second reason to want to kill me. Thankfully, a quick study of the carpet revealed no Liv-inflicted damage. *Whew.*

I spun on my heels to track the rat's trajectory across the living room. The little rodent was gunning it for a gap in the crystal perimeter. *Not today, buddy.* I lined up my arm and cracked the whip again, this time lashing the rat right in the mid-section. He let out a horrifying shriek and keeled over, dead. Two distinct colors rose from his body—one was a white wisp, the other a black swirl. I zeroed in on the black one and snapped my whip at it until the blue energy of my weapon eviscerated the darkness. When the black swirl was gone, I searched for the white wisp, only to discover it was gone, too—it had seemingly vanished into the air. Could it have been his soul? If it was, then that would have made the dark spiral . . . its *curse? Possession?*

My world shifted on its axis. I'd had a darkness trapped inside of me, and it had been a living nightmare. I'd had no control over my body, my feelings, even my own thoughts. It was like I'd been possessed. Was there any chance that was what had happened to the rat? Could the white wisp have been its once-pure soul, while the black was the darkness that controlled it? For the first time, I wondered if maybe by killing a dark-infested creature, I might actually be freeing it from a life it hadn't chosen for itself. Maybe, in a weird way, I'd just done that rat a favor.

"Great job, Allie." Greta scooped the deceased rat into the jar. She tucked the container into her bag and crossed to newly-blackened spots on the rug. "Hmm. A little help?"

"Oh, I can't heal rugs," I demurred.

"No, silly, help me move the couch. You push, I'll pull." She placed her hands on the arm of the sectional and waited for me to join her. With a shrug, I crossed to the far side and pushed. We shifted the couch six inches, until it covered the burn marks. "See?" Greta clapped her hands. "No problem."

Oh, bless her heart. She really thought Mack wouldn't notice. She had no idea he'd *feng shui*-ed that living room to within an inch of its life. He probably measured the furniture for maximum chi flow while the rest of us slept. Sooner or later, Mack would come to know that the rug had been ruined, and there would be a reckoning. I only hoped I'd be on that elusive vacation when the big day came.

"I'll go dispose of this guy, and then we can celebrate," Greta said as she skipped toward the kitchen with the rat-filled jar. The back door slammed behind her as she exited into the chilly Vancouver air. The fact that I simply watched her go was a testament to the level of weird that had become my life. *Killed a fire-breathing rat; weirdness level nine-hundred achieved.*

The Liv simmered down then, going dormant inside my chest. I lowered myself onto the newly-repositioned sectional and kicked my feet up. Accessing the Liv was always invigorating, but it usually left me exhausted, too. With a deep breath, I closed my eyes, intent on catching a moment's peace before Greta returned with her next insane training exercise. But a gust of icy wind forced my eyes open much sooner than I'd intended. Mack and Tore stepped through the front door and hurriedly closed it behind them to ebb the surge of snowflakes pushing their way into the warmth of our cabin.

"Still snowing, huh?" I pushed myself up on my elbows.

"It's coming down hard," Tore confirmed. He shot me a dimpled grin, and my cheeks warmed. *Hello, gorgeous.*

Mack stamped his feet on the doormat, then tilted his chin up to sniff the air. "What's that smell? Are you cooking again, Allie?" His eyes narrowed as he studied the room. "And did somebody move the furniture?"

My stomach clenched, and I stammered out an awkward, "Um," before I bit down on my bottom lip. Since my lying skills were abysmal, I decided to avoid the question. "I have to go to the bathroom," I blurted. Then I rushed from the room to the sound of Tore's amused chuckle.

If someone had told me a few months ago that I'd be living with four immortals and killing fire-breathing rats in my spare time, I would have thought they were crazy. Not only was that my reality, but in the morning, I'd be leaving for a realm populated by dwarves, where I'd need a magic, glowy whip to protect myself from God-only-knew what. And there was a very real chance I might die trying to retrieve the pieces of a mystical weapon from the immortal embodiment of darkness.

My life was a hot mess.

CHAPTER THREE

"BODIE, WEAPON COUNT." TORE barked his request. The guys and I were huddled in a tight circle in the snow-covered clearing in front of the safe house. The blizzard must have temporarily worn itself out—now only a light dusting of flakes fell from the heavy, grey clouds. Since we didn't know how long the reprieve would last, we needed to Bifrost out of Vancouver before the gale-force snowstorm returned. Hence, Tore's clipped demand.

"I've got a few special tools in my backpack, and everybody's got their daggers and travel weapons of choice." Bodie counted off on his fingers. "Broadswords for you and me, katanas for

Johann, a crossbow for Mack, and Allie's got her sword, her armor, and the Liv."

"Don't forget her whip," Tore added. Heat flooded my cheeks as one corner of his mouth turned up in a smirk. "Can't wait to see you get your hands on that again, Pepper."

Bodie snickered. "That's what she said."

"And, he's back." Johann rolled his eyes. "Glad Greta caught the early Bifrost out of here so we could get you back to normal."

"Shut up," Bodie muttered.

I was about to suggest that Bodie ask Greta out already, now that he was all grown-up and coordinated enough to not teeth-mash her face and all. But before I could offer my two cents, Tore jumped back into combat mode.

"Huginn's note said the dark entities were spotted due east of the Nordein range," he said. "On a slightly smaller mountain called Einermajer."

"Einer-whatter?" I muttered. Seriously, was it that hard to have normal-named mountains? Big mountain, green mountain, little mountain . . .

"Everybody suited up?" Tore looked around, and we nodded. Each of us wore what was apparently the protector traveling uniform— cargos, combat boots, and V-neck shirts, all in black, of course. We also wore a thin, waterproof, zip-up jacket over our t-shirts, and supply-laden packs on our backs. And while most of us had swords slung in holsters at our waists, I was the only one with a layer of Asgardian-issued silver covering one limb. My armor rested comfortably against my left arm, between my t-shirt and my jacket. If our previous trips had been any indicator, I'd need every advantage when we dropped into the foreign realm.

I patted my boot, where my favorite dagger was tucked snugly beside my ankle. "Let's get a move on."

"Heimdall!" Tore looked skyward. "Send down the Bifrost!"

We stepped closer together as a fierce wind whipped the snow in a tight tornado, and a burst of colors filled the clearing. Tore wrapped a protective arm around my shoulders while I tucked my face against his chest. My back still got pelted with snow, but at least my cheeks were free of the icy flakes that whirled upward. Plus, I got to smell Tore's jacket. Pine and winter and spearmint and *yum.*

"Grab on to me, Allie. And bend your knees when we land!" Tore yelled over the roar of the rainbow. I threw my arms around his chest, and he tucked me to his side. He held on tight as the Bifrost pulled us upward, away from the safe house, and into the atmosphere. My bones threatened to shoot right out of my skin as the transport rocketed us through the sky. It slowed just long enough to drop us unceremoniously over what I hoped was our destination. My knees buckled as my feet hit the ground, the jarring sensation sending shards of pain up my legs. I bit the inside of my cheek to keep from crying out as blades of agony pierced my shins from the inside out. The blades jabbed harder as I crumbled to the ground, landing hard on my butt.

"Ouch!" I yelped.

"You okay?" Tore bent down beside me, concern lining his normally-stoic features.

Between the Bifrost-induced nausea and the nearly shattered tailbone, I most certainly was *not* okay. The gently rolling hills and blossoming trees of Nidavellir swam in and out of my pain-blurred vision, and it took half a minute before I realized there was a massive, jagged mountain range resting somewhere behind them. I blinked forcefully, willing the sea of greens and greys to come into focus. At the same time, I tried *really hard* to not throw up. The entire bottom half of me was in unbelievable pain.

"Allie?" Tore's pitch went up a note. "Can you hear me? Mack, run a medical scan on her. Make sure she's all right."

"No, I'm fine." I forced myself to focus, and the pain rushed back. *Crap.* I took a slow breath, willing the unpleasant sensations to *get the hell out, already.* "Or, I will be, right after my super healing kicks in and fixes the shin splints. Or whatever's making my legs feel like they're— ouch!" I sucked in air through my teeth. "Like they're on fire."

Beside me, Mack shook his head at Tore. "You should have carried her in."

"She has to learn to Bifrost on her own. What if we have to evacuate her solo from one of these little pleasure trips?" Tore glared at Mack, but he brought his hands down to cup my lower leg. The pain ebbed slowly, but it was enough to let me breathe normally again. Some Asgardians were born with the natural inclination to heal, but from what I'd gathered, the healing gene had mostly skipped Tore. Thankfully, he seemed to have picked up a few abilities from growing up with his healer mom—like fixing Bifrost-induced shin splints.

"Teach her to land in Asgard or Alfheim," Johann chided. "Nidavellir's a borderline realm— with all the darkness that's touched it, our bodies are averse to the atmospheric impact."

"No, he's right. I need to learn to do things for myself. Especially if—" My breath caught as I broke off, my physical pain giving way to life-preserving fear. "Wait, did you say *borderline* realm?"

"It's okay, Allie," Bodie assured me. "Johann's just talking about the dragons."

He's what now?

I scrambled to my feet as my mind filled with the nightmarish image of fire breathers considerably larger than the one that had wreaked havoc on Mack's living room rug. Fire breathers with barbed tails, scales, and in all likelihood, wings.

Oh, hell to the no.

"It's okay; the dragons are good here, Allie," Bodie reassured me.

"Well, most of the time," Mack corrected.

My stomach lurched. What did he mean *most of the time?* I wrapped my hand around the hilt of my barely-still-sheathed sword and spoke through gritted teeth. "Somebody better start explaining the mostly-good dragons to me. *Real fast.*"

Johann turned in a slow circle in the clover-strewn grass. He scanned the hills, the mountains, and the tree-dusted open space behind us. He was either stalling for time or searching the skyline for the dragons that threatened to push my sanity right off the crazy cliff. "We're secure," he said, before turning to me with open arms. "Here's the deal. There are two breeds of dragons—"

"There are about fifty breeds of dragons," Mack interjected.

"I'm simplifying," Johann huffed. "Fine, there are two *varieties* of dragons. Light dragons and dark dragons."

"You really don't understand the biology behind them, do you?" Mack sighed.

Johann moved to stand in front of my lumberjack friend. His positioning prevented him from viewing Mack's pointed head shake. "The dark dragons live in Helheim—they work for Hel, the ruler of the underworld, and do pretty much whatever demonic deed she orders them to do. You don't have to worry about those dragons here. The dwarves kill them if they ever try to enter Nidavellir."

"Dwarves kill dragons?" My voice was barely a squeak as anxiety churned in my gut. Apparently, the Norse dwarves were the polar opposite of their diamond-mining, cheerful-singing, animated Midgardian cousins.

"They have to," Tore interjected. "They can't have the dark ones infecting the native dragons."

Of course not. Silly me.

"The dragons that live here are on the side of the light," Bodie chimed in. "They have allegiance to Nidavellir, Asgard, Midgard, and Vanaheim."

"Dragons have allegiances?" I questioned.

"Dragons are fiercely loyal." Johann ran his hands over the black spikes of his hair. "Legend has it the Alfödr created the original race of dragons to be guardians of the light. But darkness infiltrated a handful of the creatures, and when the Alfödr tried to cut the darkness out of them, two orbs emerged from each affected dragon—one white, one black. The Alfödr tried to eradicate the dark orbs, destroy them like we destroy the black energy that seeps from the night elves when they die. But the orbs moved too quickly. They morphed into two distinct spherical masses, creating two mega-balls of darkness. Those two balls entered the bodies of the two strongest dragons—one male, one female. The white orbs returned to the remainder of the beasts, and their descendants—the light dragons—now populate Nidavellir. Those are the dragons from human myths—the ones whose scales have magical, healing properties."

Ice-like fear danced along my spine, and my hand flexed against my sword. I was *so* not interested in a tombstone that boasted *Death by Dark Dragon*. "What happened to the dragons who got the black orbs?"

"Hel summoned those two dragons to Helheim and cultivated the darkness within them. Two grew to four, then eight, and now her realm is populated with a race of black-hearted fire breathers." Johann crossed his arms and looked Mack in the eye. "A race comprised of multiple, genome-spliced species. Not just two. Happy?"

"I suppose." Mack shrugged.

I shuddered. Johann's talk of the two orbs rising from the affected dragons reminded me of what I'd seen when I killed that rat. Maybe I really had put it out of its darkness-induced misery.

Tore cupped his hand around mine and pushed my sword back into its sheath. I hadn't realized I'd begun to pull it out. "If you kids are done with your little science chat, we need to get moving. Mount Einermajer is a half-day's hike from here, and we didn't call in our arrival."

"Meaning?" I narrowed my eyes.

"Meaning, we didn't want to alert anyone that we had a lead on the next piece of Gud Morder, so we didn't tell the dwarves we were coming. So, they didn't tell the dragons we were coming. But we can sure as *skit* assume they saw the Bifrost drop in, and they'll be here soon to investigate." Tore tightened the straps of his backpack.

Oh, God.

"But we're coming from Midgard; we're on their side. That means they're loyal to us, right?" Hope laced my tone.

"*Ja.* But dragons aren't big interrogators. They won't ask for our passports; they'll just kill us on sight when they see us with all of our weapons." Tore shrugged. "Their job is to protect, and 'strike first, ask questions later' is the safest strategy for their realm."

Fan-freaking-tastic.

I adjusted my own backpack and marched determinedly forward. "Then let's go scale Mount Einstein."

"Uh, Allie?" Bodie spoke up from behind me.

"Mmm?"

"Mount *Einermajer* is that way."

I glanced over my shoulder, where my four protectors wore looks of barely-contained amusement. Bodie pointed to a green-covered mountain range that was much too far in the distance for my liking.

"Right-o." I did an about-face and marched in the opposite direction. My boots dug into the earth as I made my way across the field of dewy clovers, past my protectors, and toward the mountain I still could not pronounce. When none of the guys matched my pace, I turned around and walked backwards. The four of them stood still, covering their grins with their hands. "What?"

"That way." Bodie's arm hadn't moved.

I followed the sight-line of his finger and realized the mountain he pointed at was a few degrees to my left . . . and considerably higher than the one I'd been heading toward. *Fabulous.* I planted my boots in the clovers and stared down the peanut gallery. "Fine. One of you trailblazers want to lead the way? Since you clearly know where you're going?"

"I'll do it." Tore snuffed his grin and jogged forward until he stood at my side. Mack followed at a more dignified pace. "You ready?" Tore asked.

I planted my hands on my hips and resumed my backward walk. "I am, but I don't know what's holding them up." I jutted my chin at the still snickering Bodie and Johann. "What are you guys waiting for? Get your butts over here. It's time to hunt down another piece of Gud Morder."

****

Three hours into our four-hour hike, I started working on my pitch to get a secondary Protector Palace in Nidavellir. The countryside was absolutely *gorgeous*. With its rolling green hills, fields of yellow flowers, and small caves tucked into the mountains, the realm reminded me of pictures I'd seen of Ireland. Our walk had been blessedly uneventful, and I was mentally congratulating our team on what was looking like an easy retrieval.

Naturally, that was when we stumbled across two limp feet sticking out from beneath an enormous boulder.

Crap.

At the sight of the lifeless feet, my protectors circled around me and drew their weapons. Tore held up a fist, and we all went perfectly still, save for the corpse-induced nausea that swirled violently in my gut. After a beat, Tore pointed to the ground. He crouched low, creeping on bent legs toward the boulder, with Mack, Johann, Bodie, and me in tow. The churning in my stomach increased as we drew upon the large, grey stone. The legs still hadn't moved, and they produced nothing by way of an energy signature—their owner was very clearly dead.

Oh, God.

I clutched my stomach, willing it to retain its contents, while Mack and Johann dropped their weapons and shoved their hands beneath the boulder. Strain lined their faces as they struggled to overturn it.

"A little help?" Johann grunted.

Tore sheathed his sword before stepping in, adding his considerable strength to the endeavor. The three of them overturned the stone, revealing a red-haired dwarf with garishly grey skin and a cloak covered in blood. The enormous gash across his neck made it clear his throat had been sliced before someone had deposited a massive rock on top of him. The dwarf's eyes faced heavenward, frozen open.

I turned away from my protectors and bent over to rest my elbows on my knees. Deep breaths did little to stop the bile sloshing in my gut or the anxiety gripping my heart. But they did ground me enough to remember that whoever killed this dwarf could very well be nearby. And we needed to move. Fast.

"Is this normal for this realm? Are there . . . dwarf bandits?" I turned back to my protectors but kept my eyes off the bloodied corpse.

Tore shifted his gaze from left to right. His nostrils flared as he drew a long breath, and his sword was back in his hands before I could blink. "It was the night elves," he hissed. "Mack?"

Mack nodded in confirmation. "They were definitely here."

My energetic grounding promptly disappeared. *RIP, grounding.* "You can smell them?" I squeaked.

"I smell evil and sulfur. Don't you?" Mack picked up his bow.

"No." I shivered. "But if you pick up the scent of sheer, unadulterated terror, don't worry. That's just me."

In an instant, the guys re-formed their tight barrier around me. Their weapons were drawn, and they looked uncharacteristically uneasy.

"We've got another hour before we reach the mountain. We'll be sitting ducks." Bodie scanned the horizon. Beside him, Mack breathed slowly in and out, no doubt trying to meditate his way out of this nightmare. Tore stared at a crop of boulders about sixty yards ahead, while Johann broke formation to kneel beside the dwarf. His rough hand ran along the decedent's face, gently closing the fallen dwarf's eyes.

"Rest in peace, brother," he said softly.

My heart squeezed with affection. Tore stepped over to pat Johann's back, then bent to pick up a golden horn that lay a few feet away. The instrument was about six inches long, etched with intricate detailing, and looked to be made of solid gold.

"What's that?" I asked nervously. If it in any way connected us to this dwarf's killer, I was ripping it out of Tore's hands and chucking it in the nearest blooming tree.

Tore slipped the horn into his pocket. "The victim was a dragon master. They carry these instruments to call their charges. Each horn's pitch is unique to the animal it summons. This man's dragon will respond to the call of this horn."

A dragon master. Holy hell. If it wasn't for the fact that we were standing next to a dead body, in imminent danger of suffering the same fate at the hands of some crazy night elves, I'd have asked a *lot* more questions. As it was, I asked only one.

"Why are you picking up his horn? We do *not* want a dragon showing up here." I blinked at the calm expressions of my clearly insane protectors. "We do not want a dragon showing up here," I reiterated. If the guys thought otherwise, I was calling Heimdall and hightailing it back to Canada solo.

"You're thinking a dragon might be our emergency exit plan, aren't you?" Bodie asked.

Tore simply nodded.

Oh, come *on.* They had to be kidding me.

"Allie, we're going to do a bit of running now. You good with that?" Tore sounded calm, but the worry lines framing his eyes let me know he was every bit as freaked out as I was. We were totally exposed and apparently on the verge of summoning an escape dragon. On purpose.

"I'm good with the running." My gaze settled on Tore's pocket, where he'd hidden the dragon-phone. "It's your extraction plan I'm not okay with."

"Just trust me." Tore sheathed his sword and took off at a jog. Was he seriously pulling the trust card? *Whatever.* With a huff, I followed him in the direction of the mountain. Crops of boulders sprung up at intervals along the hills, and we hugged their lines for shelter when we could. But for much of our trip we were completely in the open, easy pickings for any observing night elves. Each time the thought crossed my mind, I picked up my pace. By the time we were halfway to our destination, I was flat out sprinting. My feet hit the ground in rhythmic strides, each step striking the clovers with enough force to slam my backpack against my lower back. I didn't complain—none of us did. We needed to find that weapon piece before the monster who'd stricken down the dwarf found us . . . or before somebody pulled the evac card and whipped out the gold-horn-of-doom.

It was all fun and games until somebody called in the dragon.

A shriek from the sky brought our sprint to an abrupt halt. My neck tweaked as I wrenched my gaze skyward, where a large silhouette passed across the sun. It had massive wings, a long neck, and what looked suspiciously like a mace at the end of its thick tail.

"I'm hoping that's one of the friendly dragons?" I croaked.

"Get to the boulders!" Tore barked.

He didn't have to tell me twice. I lowered my head and raced for cover, pumping my arms back and forth like my life depended on it. In all likelihood, it probably did. I sent a silent prayer to whatever deity I was supposed to be praying to these days that I didn't die in a dragon-induced, demigod inferno. And I threw one more wish into the cosmos, just for good measure.

Dear Universe, Please don't let the dragon flambé my hair, either. Or any other part of me. Xoxo, Allie.

The wind behind me picked up, sending my long hair over my shoulder. When it covered my face, I ceased arm pumping to pull strands from my eyes, all the while wishing I'd had the foresight to choose braids before embarking on a recon mission. *Lesson learned.* A fierce flapping sounded directly behind me, and I sent the universe a second request, this one asking that the flapper be a previously undiscovered species of giant, benevolent butterfly.

Apparently, the universe was on a donut break.

"Allie!" Tore shouted. He'd reached the boulders ahead of me and now looked up in horror.

I spun around on my heels as an honest-to-God dragon landed directly in front of me. A freaking dragon. The beast was beautiful and terrifying all at the same time. He was a kaleidoscope of blues, with the navy scales atop his back fading down his sides to a crystalline teal at the chest. His eyes were emerald green with pure black slits for pupils, and his nostrils puffed white smoke as the creature huffed in my direction. He lowered his head to the ground and sucked in a deep breath. The air around me chilled. As did my blood.

"Should I be freaked out that he's *sniffing* me?" I whisper-screamed over my shoulder.

"Probably," came Bodie's muttered reply. "Be careful, Allie."

Without thinking it through, I flared the Liv in my chest and ran it down my arms. It only took a second to mold the light whip into shape, and I brandished it determinedly at the fire breather. If this dragon was anything like the rat from yesterday, I knew how fast he would be able to shoot flames. And I wasn't about to let Big Blue roast me or any of my friends. *Bring it on, dragon.*

The light from my whip reflected in the dragon's eyes, and the black slits of his pupils blazed blue for the briefest of moments. With a snort, the beast lowered its head. He kept his head tilted down and his eyes to the ground as he walked toward me. Either the dragon was putting on an act, or he was trying to let me know I was running this little meet-and-greet.

Or, he was just getting close enough to eat me.

"What's he doing?" I hissed at Tore without pulling my eyes from the twenty-foot-tall monster.

"Not sure," he hissed back. "Keep that whip live, Pepper."

"You think?" I muttered.

When the dragon was directly in front of me, he bent his front legs in a sort of a kneel. He turned his head so his cheek rested on the clovers, and his eyes blinked up at me with surprising warmth. He looked like he was either presenting himself for my approval or wanting me to climb on his back and ride him. Was he insane? Could I even do that? *Hold up, Allie. Do you even want to?*

Curiosity clubbed fear over the head and chucked it into one of the nearby caves. I was *totally* going to pet that dragon. And quite possibly take him for a spin. I was officially out of my mind.

"Back away slowly, Allie." Tore's voice sounded closer now. He must have snuck up behind me.

"I don't want to," I whispered.

The dragon's head snapped up at the sound of Tore's words. He reared on his hind legs and shot a fierce stream of fire just above my head. I fell backwards into Tore's thick arms.

"*Skit,*" Tore swore. He threw an arm around my chest and muscled me to the ground, pinning me beneath his massive frame. My cheek hit the clovers hard, and from the corner of my eye, I caught a blur of movement as Mack raced forward. Somehow, he'd gotten hold of the horn. He put it to his lips and blew, emitting a sharp tone that echoed off the mountaintops.

The dragon whipped his neck around at the noise. He let out a fearsome roar and spread his wings before flying high into the sky.

"Are you crazy, Allie? Please tell me you were not about to touch that thing." Tore pulled me up.

"I . . ." I didn't have an answer. I'd obviously had a fit of temporary insanity. Who the hell tried to touch a dragon? Or worse, ride one?

Mack nudged me forward, horn still in hand. "Let's move. Blowing a dragon's horn in the face of another member of its species is an act of aggression. We're lucky the one who took off seemed partial to you, but it may yet return to challenge me. Besides, the dragon I just called will be here soon. And unless it happens to be related to the other one, it will be fairly agitated when it picks up the blue dragon's scent."

Great. So, dragons were territorial. And, apparently, they knew whose horn was whose. Mack sounding the dragon-phone must have tipped off Big Blue that someone else would be coming, hence the quick departure. *So much for my dragon ride.*

"Which way?" I asked.

"Head to the mountain. Don't stop until you get there, no matter *what* happens. Understand?" Tore's command came out all growly. His long hair was a tangled mess beneath his snug, black beanie, and ordinarily, I would have taken a moment to appreciate the sexy display of dominance. Or the fact that, after *weeks* of waiting, I'd finally found myself pinned beneath Tore's tight body—albeit only to avoid death by dragon. But I was too preoccupied with not becoming reptile fodder to do more than give a curt nod.

"Understood." I took off at a sprint with my protectors on my heels. It took longer to reach the mountain than I was comfortable with, and while the dragon Mack summoned seemed to be taking its time showing up, I kept nervous eyes on the sky. We didn't stop running until we'd reached a damp, dragon-free cave at the base of Mount Ein-whatever. For a merciful, terror-free moment, I was able to catch my breath inside the silent, rocky sanctuary.

And then the dwarf arrived.

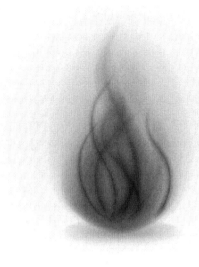

CHAPTER FOUR

"SHOW YOURSELF, KARVIR. YOUR dragon circling Mount Einermajer. She frantic, search for you." The deep, guttural voice shouted from outside the cave. It sounded gravely. And intense. And furious. So, the fallen dwarf's name had been Karvir. *May he rest in peace.*

"What's the call?" Bodie whispered to Tore. "Converse or kill?"

Kill? So much for this being a friendly realm. The poor dwarf was just trying to figure out who blew on his friend's dragon-phone. He obviously didn't know his buddy was deceased.

"I'll deal with the dwarf." Tore grimaced. "If he hasn't found his dead friend yet, he might believe we're on his side and help us."

"Or he might take one look at your resting angry face and think you killed his kin." Mack shot Tore a look. "I'll go with you. And I'll do the talking."

Tore bristled. He opened his mouth, and I was sure he was about to unload some choice words on our friend. But the dwarf resumed his shouting outside our cave-sanctuary, and Tore gave in with a resigned nod. "Fine. You lead. Johann and Bodie, stay here, and guard Allie."

"Or I'll guard them," I countered. *Girl power.*

"That too."

Mack tucked his bow over his shoulder and walked out of the cave, palms facing upward in the universal sign of 'don't shoot me with your dwarf weapon.' Tore gave a mighty eye roll but sheathed his sword and mimicked the pose. I inched my way toward the opening so I could peek out without being seen. So long as Mack did the talking, they might both make it out alive. I hoped.

Outside, Mack and Tore walked slowly toward a red-haired dwarf that could have been Karvir's twin. He had the same long hair and scraggly beard, and his own golden horn was tucked into a pouch attached to his leather belt. But unlike

Karvir, who now slumbered in eternal tranquility, this dwarf was three and a half feet of live fury.

Anxiety resumed its grip on my heart. I knew Tore and Mack could take the dwarf if it came to it. But we'd *just* escaped a dragon, and God only knew what other creatures lurked outside of our cave. Pacifying an angry dwarf did *not* fit in with our drama-free exit strategy.

Though these days, what did?

I poked my head further out of the cave. Though I kept myself hidden from view, I was still able to see my two most disparate protectors approach the dwarf. They were a study in contrasts—one a bearded, lumberjack yogi, and the other a massive bundle of pure Asgardian irritation. The dynamic duo neared the dwarf, each bringing completely different approaches to the introduction table.

This promised to be interesting.

The dwarf warily eyed my protectors as they moved toward him. When Tore's combat boots crunched on some loose rocks, the smaller creature whipped out his weapon and brandished it in front of him with a growl.

"Greetings from Alfhiem." Mack held his voice in Zen mode, as if he led a guided meditation. I knew his low tones were meant to calm everyone listening in, and maybe they would have, had Mack's audience been human. But instead of

Namaste-ing with my protectors, the dwarf pulled his attention away from Mack, looked Tore square in the eye, and spat at the ground in front him.

"Greetings from Asgard." Tore spoke through clenched teeth. In typical Tore fashion, he was as un-Zen as possible.

Mack dropped to one knee, presumably to make himself less imposing, and pulled out the golden horn. "We found your friend near the boulders, dead. He smelled of night elves. We're here to retrieve an object we believe is hidden atop this mountain and to help you avenge your fallen comrade."

The dwarf made a strangled noise as he stumbled backward. "Karvir?" He looked out into the valley in disbelief. Then his eyes fell on the horn in Mack's hand. "This is ruse! My brother strongest dwarf I know. Nothing best him—not even night elf." His clipped speech came in sharp gasps.

Bodie stepped out of the cave. "It's not a ruse. I can show you."

The dwarf eyed Bodie wearily.

"I'm not going to hurt you, I swear." Bodie held his hands a foot apart, shooting waves of energy between them. "You'll be able to witness what we saw of your brother right here. Then, you can go with us up the mountain to kill the dark elves hiding there. Or you can refuse and . . ." Bodie let the implication hang in the air.

"And you'll die like your brother," Tore offered. Mack struck his leg out, kicking Tore in ankle.

The dwarf's face scrunched up in distaste, and I wondered if he was going to spit at Tore's feet again. Instead he glared at the Asgardian and seethed. "You just like father. Things no change. Ever."

The words seemed to suck all the air from the space. Tore froze, his chest caving inward as if he'd been stabbed in the heart. My stomach plummeted in a sickening free fall as I took in his haunted eyes, slackened jaw, and the way the rest of our group looked at him with . . . was it pity? How did this dwarf know the God of Revenge? How did he know Tore?

With a tip of his head, the dwarf motioned Bodie forward. "Play your memory."

Just like that? He was willing to trust Bodie? Either this dwarf knew something about my protector I hadn't the first time Bodie had memory-balled me, or he genuinely believed Tore intended to kill him. *Poor guy.*

Bodie pulled his hands apart, and the image of Karvir pinned beneath the boulder flickered between them. As the rest of the scene played out, I fought the urge to step closer to Tore and squeeze his hand, give him a gentle hug, anything. He'd told me he wanted nothing to do with Revenge, and though his energy remained closed off, I knew the dwarf's comment had cut him deep. I wished I could help him somehow. It was hard to see him hurting.

The memory of Karvir's bloodied body faded to black between Bodie's hands. A silent tear fell down the dwarf's face as he wiped snot onto his sleeve. "Dark activity surround mountain for days. Handful of assassin dwarves went up hill to investigate. Most dragon masters clear out. Karvir and I want nothing to do with it. Took our dragons home. Thought safe."

He looked crestfallen, his mud-colored eyes and bulbous nose dripping tears and snot. Even though the dwarf had hurt Tore, he clearly grieved the loss of his brother. Resting my palms to my sides, I took a step forward and emerged from the cave. Johann followed close behind, but I waved him back and continued toward the dwarf. As I moved, I scanned his energy from his head downward. A gaping, black mass had settled over his heart center, leeching the color from the vibrant, green energy beneath. It wasn't the black of dark magic that I'd sensed in the night elves. This shade was different. It was organic, self-inflicted. The dwarf was in mourning.

A warmth built in my chest, and without thinking, I stopped directly in front of the heartbroken creature. I ran the pulse down my arm until my hand glowed with the Liv. The dwarf's mouth formed a circle, and he looked from my blue hand-ball to my eyes, then back again. Recognition dawned, and he dropped to one knee and bowed his head. "Blessings, goddess." After a pause, he stood, looking up at me with a vulnerable gaze.

My throat pinched with emotion. There wasn't anything I could do to bring his brother back, but I could do something to ease his suffering. It was all I could offer, but it would have to be enough.

"Allie, what are you doing?" Tore wrapped his fingers around my wrist, but I pulled free with a head shake.

"Healing," I said. I knelt before the dwarf, so we were almost eye to eye. His pain was so raw it nearly overwhelmed me. Instead of walking away, I strengthened my protective bubble and held up my hand. The glowing, blue ball reflected in the dwarf's muddy eyes. "May I?" I asked.

The dwarf grunted his consent, and I placed the Liv over his chest. The creature's breath hitched as the blue entered his energy. It coated the blackness like a salve, diminishing the vacuous darkness until it became a light grey, then a wispy white. Green pulsed faintly beneath the filmy layer of sorrow, and I knew that someday the dwarf's heart would be as vibrant as it had once been. A tear rolled down the creature's face, and he reached his hands up to clutch mine. His eyes shone with gratitude.

"I'm so sorry for your loss," I replied. I genuinely was.

Now that his heart was no longer heavy with mourning, he managed to give a small smile. "Karvir with gods now. Cause much mayhem, no doubt."

"No doubt." I smiled back.

"Thank you, goddess. I owe you debt." The dwarf spoke in earnest. "How I repay for healing?"

"Well," I paused, looking around at my protectors. "We don't know the mountain very well. And apparently, my friend here summoned your brother's dragon. We need to get the relic we came for and get out of your realm as soon as possible. Any chance you'd be willing to help us track it down? Please?"

The dwarf bowed his head. "It be my honor."

I reached behind me to elbow Tore in the ribs. "See what happens when you ask nicely?"

Tore cleared his throat. I turned my head, expecting to find an annoyed and impatient demigod. But what I saw sent a surge of emotion straight through my heart. Tore's haunted expression was gone, replaced by a look of utter adoration. *No freaking way.* Tore Vidarsson, a real-life demigod and my own personal source of infinite irritation, was looking at me like I was the only girl in the world. The tenderness in Tore's eyes sent my heart galloping nearly out of my chest. While I struggled to breathe, he just stared at me with an all-consuming look that pushed everyone else from my consciousness. The world shrank to our single, shared connection. He might not have been able to let his wall down enough to show me his energy, but in that moment, I knew exactly what I meant to Tore.

Holy mother of pearl. I was Tore's everything.

And I knew, without a doubt, that he was my everything, too.

****

Our little group wasted no time embarking on our mountain trek. Between the murderous night elves and the flying dragon, time was literally of the essence in tracking down the next piece of Gud Morder. Since none of us had eaten in the past four hours, Mack dug into his pack and passed around little pouches of dried fruits and nuts. We scarfed the calories and chased them down with what was left of our water to stay hydrated. Night elves and dragons would be the least of our worries if we died of starvation scaling the mountain.

Our dwarf guide, whose name turned out to be Milkir, was quite helpful. He and Mack led us in two lines up the narrow path, all the while comparing notes on the recent political upheaval in Nidavellir. Johann and Bodie took the middle, while Tore and I followed a little way behind the group. There was something I wanted to talk to Tore about, and I needed privacy to do it.

Tore raised one blond eyebrow as I laced my fingers through his and tugged him backward. "What's up?"

"How did the dwarf know who I was? Who you were?" I whispered.

Tore scowled at Milkir's back. "Dwarves have their own powers. You know they forge weapons for the gods, right?"

Nope. I definitely did not know that.

"They created Thor's hammer, Mjölnir, and his belt, Megingjörd. They even crafted Odin's golden ring, Draupnir. It self-replicates, creates eight new rings every ninth night. Mortals have waged wars trying to retrieve it," Tore continued.

I did not know that either.

"But they're also a very intuitive species. They can sense which realm a foreigner comes from, and they're able to determine what gifts an individual possesses just by looking at them.

That's why Milkir took Bodie's vision at face value—he understood it wasn't a ruse after all, but simply Bodie's gift." Tore used the hand not wrapped in mine to rub the back of his neck.

"Wow," I murmured.

"Milkir may have suspected you were a healer, but he wouldn't have known you had the Liv if you hadn't shown him. So far as the realms understand, the Liv is trapped in the Night Sleep with your mother. Nobody knew it could transfer so long as its host was still alive. You shocked the Hel out of us with that one." Tore shot me a wink. "But when you used it on him, he knew exactly what it was. All species do. It's legendary."

"No pressure, huh?" I let out a nervous chuckle. "But how did he know who you are? He mentioned your father. What was up with that?"

Tore's eyes darkened to a smoky blue. "Once upon a time, the God of Revenge brought a needless war to Nidavellir. Many dwarves were massacred. Things like that aren't easily forgotten."

"Oh, Tore." I squeezed his hand lightly. No wonder he didn't want anything to do with Revenge. My heart tugged as I imagined the pain his father's legacy continued to cause him. But there was something else I needed to ask, and while I knew it was hard to talk about, I also knew I might never get a better opening. My voice was barely audible as I looked up at Tore and asked, "What happened between you and your dad?"

Tore's boots skidded on the rocks as he came to an abrupt stop. He slowly pivoted to face me with eyes cloudy from barely-contained emotion. A thick blanket of closeted pain broke through Tore's protections to descend on me. *Crap.* Was he mad that I'd asked? Had I pushed him too far? God, had I just reopened a wound he'd spent who knows how long trying to close? My heart thundered against my ribcage for a half minute, slowing only when Tore brought his hands up to cup my face. He held my cheeks tenderly before tangling his fingers in my hair.

"All you need to know is that my father took away the one bright light I had in my life. He snuffed it out, and I was left in darkness for years." Tore leaned forward and brushed a light kiss on my lips. "Until now."

The heavy blanket lifted, my anxiety giving way to a soft glow. My heart warmed with a joyful energy that grew until sparkly luminescence shot through my bubble. "Tore," I whispered.

"You're my light now," he murmured. He laced one hand through mine and moved forward again, leaving me to catch my breath as I stumbled after him. Sure, technically he'd avoided the question— he hadn't actually told me what happened with him and his dad. But he had opened up. He'd called me his light. That was pretty freaking awesome.

By the time we caught up to the rest of our party, they'd nearly reached the summit. The guys were crouched behind an outcropping of boulders, their attention focused on something behind the rocks. Bodie held one finger to his lips, and I picked up the gravelly tones of a heated argument, along with the heavy energy that seeped from only the darkest of souls.

It looked like we'd found our night elves.

"Hurry up and open the portal!" a snarly voice hissed. "The girl will arrive any moment, and I want that bounty."

"Opening a portal in a light realm isn't easy!" the second voice spat back.

Tore's hand clamped down on mine so hard, I nearly yelped. He pulled me closer to him while crunching rocks above us drew my attention up. As I craned my neck toward the summit, I sucked in a sharp breath.

This mission had just gone from bad to *way freaking worse.*

"Tore," I whispered. "Tell me I'm imagining that thing."

"You're not imagining it," he whispered back.

Crap.

Tore and I held hands as a black dragon with glowing red eyes stared down at us. Calculation flared in those fiery slits, and I had zero doubt it intended to eat me. This was *so* not the same kind of dragon I'd met before. Big Blue had wanted a belly rub; Black was fixing to floss his teeth with me. And what Blue offered in invitation, Black doubled down in repulsion. This beast was absolutely crawling with thick, dark energy. Ice-like fear skittered across my back. Black was definitely bad news. We had to get out of here, and *fast.*

Before we could do anything to warn the rest of our team, the dragon tipped his head back and roared. A stream of fire filled the air, singeing the trees that lined the mountaintop and alerting the night elves to our presence.

"Retreat!" Mack yelled. He didn't have to ask me twice. I turned around and bolted back down the hill, away from the dragon that now flapped toward us. We hadn't made it twenty yards when the dragon landed on the path in front of us, blocking our escape route.

"Un-retreat!" I screamed, turning and running back *up* the hill. Mack, Bodie, Johann, and Milkir raced up the path, but Tore didn't move.

"Go ahead of me, Allie," Tore shouted as I raced by him. "I'll hold it off." Tore drew his sword and brandished it at the dragon.

"No way." I skidded to a stop. "I'm not letting that thing turn you into charred demigod."

"It's not going to hurt me," Tore argued. "I've slain a lot of dragons in my day. I can take a weakling like this one."

The dragon snorted twin fireballs. *Weakling, yeah right.*

"Are you kidding me? Your hair will go up in flames in two seconds flat. The guys can handle the elves—I'm not leaving you alone." I drew my sword and took my place at Tore's side. Our blades glowed blue as the souls of Valhalla's finest infused them with their power. We stepped slowly toward the dragon, moving our swords in unison. The beast's eyes zeroed in on the whirling blue lights, and he emitted another set of fireballs from his nostrils. He dug his taloned feet into the rocky trail and puffed his chest, drawing in a deep breath.

Terror mixed with awe as the dragon reared his head back. Something about the dragon's movement was familiar—as if I'd seen it before. Obviously, I hadn't; I'd spent the majority of my eighteen years on Earth, and from what I'd seen, flame-throwing, winged beasts weren't welcome there. And Eir had seemed like someone who'd be a decent mother, not the kind to let her infant daughter play with dragons. I shook off the thought as smoke streamed from the dragon's flared nostrils.

"He's going to blow," Tore warned.

"To the left! That boulder—go!" I flung myself at Tore, pushing him behind an enormous rock as heat singed my boots.

"Allie!" Tore's fingers wrapped around my forearms. He pulled me into him, drawing me behind the boulder as a second wave of fire struck the exact spot I'd just occupied. Heat radiated at my back, and I pulled my feet to my chest to avoid unnecessary boot melting. I'd only brought the one pair on this pleasure cruise, and I hated to ruin them. Not to mention that I was kind of partial to my feet.

"New plan," Tore murmured in my ear. "We charge the dragon and just kill it. You good with that?"

I dusted the ash from my pants and stood up. "Don't know why we didn't go that route in the first place."

Not that I was dying to add dragon slayer to my resume, but I did want to survive this day.

"We won't have much time. I'll go high and aim for his throat, and you slide low and go for his gut." Tore had his battle face on. He was all clenched jaw and narrowed eyes. Everything from his shallow breaths to his bulging biceps screamed, *'I will slay you, dragon.'* It was all kinds of sexy.

"I've got your back." My words were muffled by another wave of flames crashing against the rock. *Crappers.*

Tore looked into my eyes. "I know you do."

If we weren't trying super hard to avoid being flambéed by a dragon, I would have kissed him.

"Go!" I shouted. We burst from behind the boulder and charged at the winged beast. Tore darted ahead of me. He leapt into position directly in front of the dragon, dug his heels into the ground, and took a steady stance as he raised his sword high. In one swift movement, he gouged the dragon's neck with his glowing blade. While he distracted the beast via stabbing, I slid on my shins, cruising on the gravel walkway to slide around Tore. I had a running start and so much momentum that I nearly slammed right into the dragon's underside. Its stomach was so full—I did not want to think *with what*—that it nearly brushed the ground. With a heavy exhale, I slammed my blade into the dragon's gut. It pierced a tender spot right between two scales, and the dragon fell backward with a roar. As it tumbled, smoke leaked from the hissing hole in its stomach. Tore leapt on top of the injured dragon's body and finished him off with fierce thrusts of his sword. The whole experience was like witnessing a car wreck—I didn't want to watch Tore gut the creature, but I couldn't stop myself. Sweat and blood quickly covered Tore's face as he drove his sword in and out of the dragon's flesh, but he didn't stop to wipe it away. He stabbed the dragon one final time, then raised his head to give me a look. A look that said he wasn't tired and could easily kill three more fire breathers should they decide to present themselves.

My boyfriend had literally slayed a dragon. It was official: Tore Vidarsson could not get any hotter.

When the dragon was still and smoke no longer seeped from its chest, Tore leapt off of its stomach and took his place beside me. "You okay, Pepper?" he asked.

"Better than you." I sheathed my sword and was about to reach up to wipe the thick goo from Tore's cheek when a dark shadow pulled my attention back to the fallen dragon.

"What is that?" I jabbed my finger at the menacing black orb that floated above the deceased dragon's body.

Tore and I locked eyes as Mack's deep voice shouted from behind us. If the yogi was screaming, things definitely weren't going well. "Can you take care of the dark orb by yourself?" Tore asked.

I nodded. "Go help the guys."

Tore was off and running before I finished my sentence. A low hiss from behind forced my attention back to the approaching black orb. The darkness moved in a serpentine pattern, no doubt searching for a new host. Since I was the only living body this side of the boulders, it bore down on me, dive bombing straight for my heart.

I don't think so, darkness.

With one flick of my wrist, my light whip blazed to life. The orb abruptly halted its trajectory before trying to retreat. *Nice.* I stepped forward, pivoting my leg to gain traction against the gravel, and cracked the whip hard. The glowing rope sliced the orb in half. Its two pieces fell to the ground and twitched before rolling toward me. They were still alive? This orb was straight out of a horror movie—cut off one head, and more grew back in its place. Clearly the light-whip slice-and-dice wasn't going to get the job done. If anything, it would exponentially increase my problems. *Think, Allie. The whip didn't work, what else do you have?* A pulse at my hip reminded me of my soul-laced sword. I had no idea if Valhalla's finest could destroy the darkness, but it was worth a shot.

I quickly drew the blade with one hand and plunged it right into the center of one of the black blobs. At the same time, I used my other hand to crack the whip into the second piece. Both orbs flickered, and for one terrifying moment, I feared four would appear in their place. But the simultaneous dose of sword and whip must have had some other-worldly power, because bursts of smoke emerged from the twin orbs. Black dust coated the air while my nostrils were assaulted with sulfur. The next instant, both the smell and the smoke were gone, taking whatever remained of the orbs with them.

Thank God.

The clang of swords at my back marked the end of my victory party. With a decisive turn, I ran back up the hill to help my boys. The small stretch of gravel passed quickly beneath my boots, and I drew a sharp breath when I skidded sharply around the bend.

"Whoa," I muttered. My protectors had done some major damage in the time it had taken me to end the orb. Two night elves lay dead in front of a huge hole that swirled inches above the ground. It spun in a clockwise rotation, connecting Nidavellir to an endless abyss of blackness. "What is that?"

Bodie grunted from my right as he helped Milkir stand. "It's a portal. Heads right back to Nott, I suspect."

Portal? Why weren't we using these instead of the rainbow of doom? The Bifrost took motion sickness to a whole new level.

"Stay back, Allie. This portal is full of dark magic. See the sparks popping at its edges?" Bodie grabbed my wrist and pulled me backward. I hadn't realized I was leaning forward, but the minute I was at Bodie's side, I lost my view of the glowing red embers buried deep within the blackness. Wherever that thing led, it sure didn't look good.

"Allie!" Johann's voice echoed from somewhere beyond the trail's end. "The piece is in this cavern!"

Sure enough, the armor beneath my jacket gave a slight hum. The light vibration trailed from my cuff through my shoulder piece, holding steady in my necklace.

"Coming," I shouted, before checking in with Bodie. "You good here?"

"I'll guard this thing; you just go retrieve Gud Morder." Bodie nodded, and I raced toward the sound of Johann's voice.

"Where are you?" I rounded another bend and found myself staring at two openings in the mountainside. My armor vibrated again, sending a stronger pulse to my necklace.

"In here!" Johann's voice came from the hole on the right. *Here goes nothing.* I drew my sword and charged into the cave. Inside, Tore was helping Mack wrap his shoulder while Johann hovered protectively in front of a radiant, white light.

"You okay?" Tore asked me. His eyes moved up and down my body, either checking me out or assessing me for injuries. Both options were wins for me.

"I'm good," I assured him. We shared a tight smile as I moved past him to get to Johann.

"Let's move, Allie," Johann urged. "It's back there." Johann jutted his chin toward the bend in the tunnel, where a bright light beamed from around the corner.

"Looks like it." My armor continued to pulse as we made our way along the narrow corridor of the cave. By the time we reached the small pile of rocks that framed a blindingly bright light, the silver piece on my arm all but jumped off my skin. It wanted to bond with the next piece of Gud Morder, like, yesterday. *You and me both, armor.* Johann stepped aside, and I bent down toward the light, carefully scooping up the piece of the curved twin blades of my god-killing weapon. Its glow faded the moment it touched my hands. *Huh.* Was that its defense mechanism? Did the pieces stop glowing once they were 'captured' so I could unobtrusively smuggle them home? For that matter, did they only glow when I was around, so it would be easy for me to find them? If those night elves had seen the glow, why the hell were they sitting at the portal waiting to push me through instead of retrieving this thing and chucking it back to Nott?

"It's just laying here," I mused out loud, "and those night elves were what, fifteen yards away? Why didn't they grab it?"

Tore's voice called out from the cave opening. "I don't think they can. I don't think any of us can retrieve the pieces except you. Otherwise, you're right—those elves would have snatched it up and thrown it through the portal. Or Nott would have shown up and grabbed it herself."

"That's what I was thinking," I agreed.

"Hold up," Johann cocked his head. "Nott touched Gud Morder before, way back when she shattered it into eight pieces. Why could she touch the pieces then, but not now?"

"Huh." I rubbed my forehead. This whole scenario made zero sense. Nott knew I was after the weapon, and she knew I'd try to kill her with it—it was why Gud Morder was created in the first place. Surely if she could open a dark magic portal, she could find a way to transport one of the pieces . . . couldn't she?

Bodie's shout derailed my train of thought. "Incoming hostiles, on foot and by air!" he yelled.

Oh, no. I shoved the piece into my waist pouch, then pounded after Johann toward the mouth of the cave. Mack and Milkir faced the trail on my left. The light elf held his crossbow at the ready while Milkir pulled a blade from his belt. They brandished their weapons at the troop of night elves making their way up the gravelly mountain path at an alarming speed.

"Oh, *skit*," Johann swore. "I'll go help with the night elves. You help with *that*." I whirled to my right, where a threat even scarier than a battalion of night elves flapped directly above Tore and Bodie. My protectors stood at the edge of the mountain, swords drawn, facing an enormous, winged dragon. This one had deep, scarlet-toned scales and eyes that blazed a fiery shade of red like the monster that had tried to kill me back by the boulders. As Tore waved his sword from side to side, Red swooped down, digging enormous talons into the gravel to land at the mouth of the cave. His eyes darted from me to the portal and back before he chuffed, filling his nostrils with smoke.

"Milkir?" I called to the dwarf. "The red-eyed ones are the bad kind, right?"

"Yes," he shouted back. "But that my brother's dragon. Eyes should be green."

"They're red," I replied nervously. "And it's snuffing fire at us."

"Maybe it's possessed," Bodie muttered.

Crappers, that's a real thing?

Tore stepped in front of me and raised his sword. "Whatever happens, stay away from the portal," he warned.

"You think?" I muttered.

"Look out!" Bodie shoved Tore to the side just as an arrow pierced the air where Tore's head had been. It landed atop the dragon's front foot, and the beast gave an enormous, flame-filled roar.

"Allie!" Tore's shout startled me nearly as much as the fireball that threatened to singe my cargoes. I dropped on my stomach and rolled away, extinguishing the flame using textbook execution of the stop, drop, and roll technique I'd learned in kindergarten. I stopped just behind Bodie, who looked down for the briefest moment.

"You okay?" He kept his sword raised at the once-again chuffing dragon.

"Barely," I muttered. "You?'

"At the moment. Mack?" Bodie called out.

"Not doing so great," Mack grunted. A quick peek revealed Mack, Milkir, and Johann dodging arrows from the rapidly approaching night elves. Mack fired back, making quick shots with his crossbow. He picked off two elves before the rest took shelter behind a boulder.

"Some assistance would be nice," Johann called up. He had a katana in each hand and was batting away arrows like they were tennis balls. Those night elves were *fast*.

"Allie, you think you can work your whip magic on this dragon?" Tore asked.

My stomach dropped. "I can try," I wavered. We'd taken out the last one with swords. I wasn't sure if I had enough control over the Liv to literally whip this dragon into submission.

"Good. You and Bodie let us know if things go downhill. I'll just be over there." With that, Tore raised his sword and charged down the hill into the fray of dark energy. He hacked away at night elf limbs, seeming every bit as possessed as the dragon still snorting fire in front of me.

Oh, God, the dragon. The beast pawed the dirt like a bull about to charge. Bodie and I both had our backs to the portal, which seemed like poor tactical positioning on our part. With nowhere to retreat, we were as defenseless as a set of pins at the end of a bowling alley. And that flaming, snorting, paw-clawing dragon was *way* more indomitable than a ten-pound bowling ball. This was definitely not good.

I scrambled to my feet and stepped behind Bodie. "Do we have a plan?" I asked.

"Yeah." Bodie crouched down and held his sword at eye level. "Don't fall into the portal. Also, don't die."

"Sounds like a good plan." I drew a long breath and focused on the energy that built in my chest. When I called up the Liv, my whip immediately flared to life in my palm. Looked like necessity was the mother of weapon invention after all. *Thank God.*

The dragon swung his long neck around to stare at my whip. The glowing blue of the rope glinted against the red inferno of the creature's eyes. When he let out another stream of fire, I thrust my hand out and cracked the whip, missing the dragon's throat by a solid two feet. *Dang it. Dragon beheading fail.* Worse, what I hadn't accomplished in decapitation, I'd more than made up for in infuriating my would-be executioner. The dragon roared again, sending a searing stream of heat just above my head.

Bodie inched closer to me as I cracked my whip again. This time I nicked the dragon squarely across one eye. He howled in fury before snorting another fire stream. I jumped backward to avoid the heat and landed precariously close to the edge of the open portal. The heel of my boot nudged a few rocks over the ledge, and a jubilant hiss emerged from the hole as the rocks dropped into the blackness. *Oh, God, don't fall in.* I chanced a quick glance away from the dragon to make sure I wasn't about to embark on a one-way trip to a dark realm. But before I could make sense of the red and black blurs moving within the portal, Bodie's shout snapped my focus straight back to Nidavellir.

"Allie! Move!" he cried. His massive body soared through the air, arms outstretched as he flew at me like a linebacker. He crashed into me, knocking me away from the swirling black hole as the dragon reared up on his hind legs. The beast flapped his wings and leaned back onto his tail, lashing out with one scaly foot. His talons connected squarely with Bodie's back and flung him into the space just above the portal.

"Bodie!" I shrieked.

Everything shifted into slow motion then. My shoulder and face hit the ground, the metallic flavor of copper filling my mouth as I bit down hard enough on my tongue to draw blood. Sharp rocks dug into my cheek as I skidded across the gravel. All the while, Bodie's flailing form descended into the darkness. His feet disappeared first, then his legs and his torso. Bile filled my gut as I stared into his horror-filled eyes, and his shaking hands disappeared into the void.

Just like that, Bodie was gone.

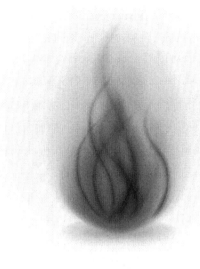

CHAPTER FIVE

"NO!" I SHRIEKED. "BODIE!" I scrambled to my feet and charged at the portal. No way was my friend going to face the darkness alone. I pushed off the balls of my feet and leapt into the air, holding my breath as I prepared to drop into the spinning black mass. But as I soared across the space that separated me from the portal, it crackled loudly and disappeared. One minute, a swirling black hole was gouged deep into the earth. The next, I landed hard on the solid, gravel path.

No. No. No!

I clawed at the earth, my fingernails digging into the rocky surface in a fruitless attempt to dig my friend out of a non-existent hole. How had this happened? How had a dragon, *a freaking possessed dragon*, kicked one of the sunniest souls I'd ever met into a black void? And how were we supposed to get Bodie back when the hole was completely and totally *missing*?

Somewhere in the haze that was my consciousness, I registered the rumble of Tore's voice and the clash of Johann's swords. But I couldn't think. Bodie was gone—*gone.* He'd taken the kick so I wouldn't have to. And if the heat at my back was any indication, the monster who'd sent my friend to God-knows-where had turned its focus onto me.

I pivoted on one heel to stare down the scaly creature. His nostrils flared as another stream shot from its nose, landing in the exact spot I'd last seen Bodie. *Screw you, dragon.* A fresh surge of anger flared the Liv to life in my chest. A furious cry tore from my lungs as I ran the energy down my arms and into my palms. I charged the dragon as my whip formed in my hand, then cracked the blue rope at the creature's head. It caught him by the throat, so I wrenched my arm behind me to force the dragon onto its knees. When he was pinned down, I freed my sword from its sheath and pierced the monster's gut. Pearlescent-colored blood spilled along the hilt to cover my hand. I didn't care that the dragon had belonged to our dwarf-guide's brother or that he had allegedly been possessed and might not be acting of his own will. The only thing I cared about was making sure the monster who sent my friend away died. *Right now.*

A blur of movement caught me off guard, and my blood-covered sword slipped out of my hand before I realized Tore was there, taking the beast down with me. His features were set in an expression of complete and total shock, and he rammed his sword in and out of the dragon with a rage that matched my own. We would end the thing that took Bodie from us. And we would do it together.

It wasn't long before the dragon keeled over on his side, life seeping out of his body while blood oozed down our arms. My rage didn't ebb until the moment the monster died, when its crimson eyes morphed to a striking emerald green before flickering to black. In that moment, I understood why Milkir had been confused when I'd said it had red eyes. Bodie had been right—the dragon hadn't been born of the darkness; it was changed. *Possessed.* The re-emergence of its emerald eyes, even for that brief moment, proved Red was more like Big Blue than the black terror Tore and I had fought down the mountain. And unlike Black, whose death had yielded just one orb of darkness that rose from his body, Red's lifeless form now had two orbs that floated just above his chest. One was black, the other blue. But the orb wasn't just blue; it was the most brilliant cerulean I had ever seen. My breath caught in my throat when I realized why the color was so familiar. It was Liv. This dragon's soul was made of the Liv. *No freaking way.*

Red was just like me on the inside, but he had been possessed by an evil entity and forced to attack. The dragon hadn't been the one who hurt Bodie—it had been the other, darker entity. Rage bubbled inside of me for a whole new reason, and I focused all of my anger on the likely culprit: Red's possession. Nott needed to die, for so many reasons.

Beside me, Tore withdrew his sword from the dragon's corpse and leaned over to put his hands on his knees. His chest rose and fell with the effort of breathing, and I knew he was barely holding it together. The black orb must have sensed his vulnerability, because it flew through the air, heading straight for Tore's heart. *Oh, hell no, orb.* With one flick of my wrist, the light whip surged in my hand. The darkness scurried backward in a hasty retreat, but I ran forward, lashing until I'd hacked the orb into tiny pieces that dissipated into the Nidavellir sky. When I was sure it wasn't coming back, I turned my attention to the blue orb. It wasn't moving. Instead, it hovered over the dragon's heart as if it wanted to go back.

Hold on. Could it go back? Was that what had happened to me when the darkness overtook me back on Jotunheim? At the time, I'd been so sucked under, I'd lost all sense of who and what I was. Had my own Liv left, then somehow been returned to my body? Could I do that for the dragon?

Purely on instinct, I reached out to touch the blue orb of the dragon's soul. At the contact, a pulse of energy ran up my arm. *No freaking way.* My Liv and his Liv were connected. The dragon and I were one.

"Allie." Tore's voice broke with raw emotion.

"We're the same," I said. There was no other way to explain it.

As I spoke the words, a fresh surge of energy hit me. A wave of sadness hit my heart, and I knew it came from the blue orb of the dragon's soul. It wasn't Red's time to die—I knew that deep within my being. And I sensed I had the power to correct what Nott had done.

Even if I had zero idea how I was going to do it.

Acting purely on instinct, I dropped my sword and placed both hands on the orb. It molded into a semi-solid mass in my two outstretched palms.

"Allie." Mack's deep voice came from my side. He must have joined Tore while I'd been communicating with the orb. I turned my senses outward, where clangs of metal let me know that Milkir and Johann continued their fight against the night elves. In all likelihood, they needed our help.

But, so did this dragon.

"I need to make it right," I told my protectors. I bent down and gently nudged the blue light against the dragon's chest. When it hit the creature's skin, the orb turned into a molten liquid. The blue flowed into the scales, through the veins, and covered the dragon's entire body in a glowing, azure hue. As seconds ticked by, the dragon's wounds began to heal. The deep cuts Tore and I had inflicted with our swords repaired themselves, the gaping wounds knitting themselves back together as I tried not to gawk. Red remained immobile. But his veins glowed beneath his scales, and his wounds shrank so they were barely noticeable. The dragon was healing— the Liv was restoring him!

A fierce wind pulled my attention to the sky. Big Blue had returned and now flapped his wings fifty yards from his comatose comrade. The dragon's green eyes studied Red; then his gaze settled on me. *Oh, God.* But any animosity Big Blue may have felt toward our party seemed to vanish as the creature hovered beyond the ledge, looking at me as if awaiting instructions. My necklace pulsed, sending a fresh surge of strength through my torso. Without thinking about how ridiculous I must have looked, I pointed to where Milkir and Johann battled the night elves and shouted a command at Big Blue. "Go help my friends!"

Big Blue bobbed his head up and down, then flapped toward the battle going on down the hill. He dove down, taking one night elf at a time in his massive jaw and crushing each with a loud crunch. In no time at all, the attack party was nothing more than a terrible memory. *Good riddance.*

A snuffing at my feet brought my attention back to Red. The glow had faded from the dragon's scales, and his eyes fluttered open. They were green again, thank God. He was free of the darkness. Red drew shallow breaths as he pushed himself onto his knees and dropped his head low in submission.

"Allie?" Mack's voice dripped with confusion. "What's going on?"

I honestly didn't know. It was Tore who chimed in with the most improbable answer imaginable.

"Allie can control them," Tore whispered.

What the hell did he just say?

We didn't have time to deal with whatever was happening with the possibly controllable dragons. Now that they weren't trying to kill us, we needed to figure out how to get Bodie back before heartbreak ended us all. I stumbled to the spot where the black hole had been and turned to Tore. "Can we reopen the portal?" I asked.

Tore shook his head, then rubbed the heels of his hands against his red-rimmed eyes. "Only dark magic can do that. And we don't have any allies who can wield it."

Grief squeezed me from the inside out. Tears pooled in my eyes as my chest rose and fell with barely-contained panic. "Where did it take him? I saw some red inside the black hole. It looked like a fire waterfall—maybe lava?"

"Sounds like Muspelheim." Mack's voice was robotic, devoid of the Zen-like peace I'd grown accustomed to.

Johann, Milkir, and Big Blue moved slowly up the pathway. The guys flanked Tore and Mack, while Big Blue knelt beside Red and lowered his head. Tore quickly brought Johann and Milkir up to date on what had happened to Bodie. I didn't bother to greet any of them. The only thing I could think about was getting our friend back.

I paced back and forth, trying to ground out my fear in measured steps. "Okay." My voice shook as I fought back tears. "We'll kidnap some dark magic users and make them re-open the portal. Or wait! Screw the portal, we can just go to Muspelheim on our own. Heimdall! Open the Bifrost." I screamed at the sky, my voice distorted by the wrenching sobs that finally escaped my gut.

Once they began, they came in earnest. And as I shouted Heimdall's name over and over, the words became one continuous wail. Hot tears streamed down my face, and I fell to my knees. Bodie was gone. It was my fault. And I had no idea how to get him back. "Please, Heimdall," I hiccupped. "Take us to Bodie."

Tore crossed the space and swept me into his arms. His hard chest pressed against mine, absorbing some of my pain. "Shh," he soothed, stroking my hair.

"He saved me," I managed between sobs. "The dragon was going for me, and Bodie pushed me out of the way. He got pushed into the portal in my place."

Tore's lips brushed against my ear as he spoke in low tones. "We can't go to Muspelheim now. Nott will be expecting us to go after Bodie, and she'll have an army waiting for us. We need more warriors. And we need the Alfödr's ravens to scout the realm to pinpoint Bodie's location. Muspelheim is a huge realm; going in blind would get us nowhere but dead. We need a plan."

"She'll kill him!" I whispered into Tore's chest.

He pulled away from me and wiped the tears from my cheeks. "No, she won't."

"How do you know that?" I desperately wanted to believe his words, but they were even more improbable than the twin dragons currently bowing at my feet.

"Because." Tore slid one hand around my lower back and closed his eyes. "Now she has the perfect bait to get you."

CHAPTER SIX

AS WE MADE OUR WAY down the mountain, my heart was nearly as heavy as it had been on Jotunheim. Logically, I understood why we couldn't follow Bodie straight to Muspelheim. But leaving him alone with the night goddess while we worked out an extraction plan was terrifying. I could only imagine the kind of torture she was putting him through in the name of interrogation, or just plain cruelty. My friend would suffer horrors beyond my wildest nightmares, simply because he'd protected me from a monster.

I couldn't wait to fuse Gud Morder and shove it through Nott's sorry excuse for a heart.

My remaining protectors, the dwarf, and I made our way down the narrow trail, with Red and Big Blue flapping their wings alongside us. Mack had told us non-related dragons were territorial, so from the way these two flew close together, I could only surmise they shared some DNA. They seemed protective of us. It was comforting to know that if we were attacked again, the dragons could straight up kill the perps before we could whip out our weapons. Or so I hoped.

As we shuffled down the hill, Milkir repeatedly turned around to shoot me curious looks. No doubt he was wondering how I'd brought his brother's dead dragon back to life. I was wondering the same thing myself. The Liv didn't exactly come with an owner's manual.

"Uh, Milkir?" I asked as the dwarf shot me his umpteenth look. "Why isn't your brother's dragon flying away? I get that yours lives with you and all, but Karvir's dragon is free now. He could leave if he wanted to. Right?"

Milkir skidded to a stop so quickly, I nearly slammed into his back. Big Blue and Red flapped backward, hovering beside us, while my protectors exchanged confused looks.

"What's going on?" Tore asked.

"I'm not sure." I turned to the scarlet-hued dragon and waved my arms in the air. "Go on!

You're free!" I called. But that only seemed to encourage the creature. Red flew closer to me, the thick lids of his eyes pulling back as if he was . . . amused?

"That no how dragons work," Milkir said. "My brother's dragon bond to him when he was child. They were one for many years. But now . . ." The dwarf pulled on my arm and stood on his toes so he could study my eyes.

"What's he doing?" I whispered to Mack.

"Just go with it," Mack whispered back.

Tore didn't seem to like the dwarf's fascination with my face. He stepped in front of me, separating us. "What's up?" he asked.

"Her eyes," Milkir whispered in awe. He turned to study Red. "And dragon—she have same eyes as girl. Look!"

Okay, so Red was a female. *My bad.*

"Look at me, Allie," Tore commanded. I stared at him, and he studied my eyes before glancing at the dragon. His brow shot up as he muttered, "Impossible."

"What's impossible?" I asked.

Milkir reached around Tore and gently touched my hand. "You bond to dragon. Animal's green eyes now streaked with blue. Your blue eyes have small green streak now."

102

"But Allie's not a dwarf. She's a demigod." Tore rubbed the back of his neck. "It's not possible for her to bond with a dragon."

"A demigod." Milkir raised his palms. "Who knows what your kind capable of?"

I backed up a step. "You're saying I'm bonded to a dragon? Through my eyeballs. Is this for real?" *Commence full-fledged nervous breakdown . . . now.*

Tore exhaled slowly. "Apparently. Not the eyeball part, but you're bonded, all right. And if what I understand about dragon culture is true, you and this red one here are bonded for life."

"What?" I screeched. My breathing grew shallow, and I wondered if I was due for another panic attack. It had been at least five minutes since the last terror-inducing incident; surely the universe owed me another reason to freak out.

Mack walked back up the hill so he stood just behind Milkir. "This is a good thing, Allie. A real honor." His yoga voice had returned.

It wasn't having the desired effect.

"I live on Earth. I can't have a pet dragon!"

Milkir scowled. "Is no pet. Is best friend. Warrior. Life partner."

"Right." I lowered my voice an octave. "I just . . . I can't have a dragon warrior life partner. Can we undo it?"

Milkir looked like I'd slapped him. "Most dragons only bond once in lifetime. This one chose you to replace my brother. She do anything for you now. You discard that?"

When he put it like that, I felt like a total jerk. "No. I'm . . . I'm honored. It's just, well, I live with humans. We don't keep dragons back home."

Milkir looked from me to Red and back before stroking his thick, crimson beard. After a moment, he snapped his fingers. "I feed her for you, let her live with me. But you come once week to fly her. Or you call her on golden horn, and she find you. Horn no have boundaries. Dragon no have boundaries, either. Her soul chose *you*," he said by way of reminder. "She bonded to *you*. Not me. Without connection to you, her soul die."

Good Lord. Now I was in charge of keeping the dragon alive? I couldn't even keep a lucky bamboo alive! And what was this about *riding* her? What we really needed to focus on was getting Bodie back from wherever Nott's portal led. This was hardly the time for animal husbandry.

Mack chose that moment to speak on my behalf. "Allie will visit weekly. And we will figure out a place to keep the creature long term. Your brother's dragon will not suffer for lack of connection."

I glared at Mack. Visions of this dragon living in the complex sent a throbbing ache through my skull.

Milkir motioned to the dragon. "She reborn. New Master. New name."

My brow furrowed. "Huh?"

Tore sighed. "He's saying you need to name her. Got any ideas?"

Oh. "Uh . . . well . . . What kinds of names do dragons usually have?"

"Dragons regal creatures, deserve regal names. Your dragon's sister—my dragon—named Drakira," Milkir offered.

Drakira? Seriously? I raised my eyebrows at Red's sister, silently apologizing for thinking she was a boy, too. She snorted a tiny fireball. *Nope.* That dragon was most definitely named Big Blue. I'd figure out a way to tell Milkir later.

"Huh. Well, what if I went with a, uh, non-regal name?" I hedged.

Milkir furrowed his brow. "Why you do that?"

"Because I'm really not that creative of a namer." And also, because I didn't want my dragon to be saddled with a name that made her sound like a reptilian pop star.

One corner of Tore's mouth quirked up in a half-smile. "What'd you have in mind?"

"Well." I glanced at my dragon. If her sister had to answer to Drakira, Red seemed almost cruelly plain. But I wasn't about to make my dragon respond to Redirka or whatever the crimson-hued equivalent of a regal dragon name would be. She needed something pronounceable, yet special at the same time. Something that suited her. Something like . . . *Scarlet?*

The thought had barely passed my mind when my dragon's head bobbed up and down. What the . . . ? Could she read my mind? No . . . surely not. She was just excited about being named. *All right, Scarlet it is.* With a grin, I turned to face our group. "Guys, I have decided her name is Scarlet."

Milkir's jaw dropped open. "Scarlet?"

I shrugged. "She likes it."

Scarlet flapped her wings, moving closer to nuzzle her head against me. She pulled back and batted her eyes at Tore, fluttering her long black lashes so they brushed against his arm. Was she flirting with him? I laughed out loud. I couldn't exactly blame her—the girl had good taste.

"Scarlet?" Milkir asked again. "Is human name."

Mack reached over the shell-shocked dwarf to touch Scarlet's neck. "Welcome, sister." He folded his hands and bowed. Our dragon closed her eyes in a seeming display of reverence.

"Scarlet," Johann said curtly. Angry red lines shot through his energy as he spoke her name.

Instinctively, I reached out to touch Johann's arm. "It's not her fault she pushed Bodie into the portal," I explained. "The darkness that was inside her controlled her consciousness. If it was anything like what I had inside me in Jotunheim, she had very little control over her actions. Or even her thoughts."

Johann gave a tight nod. His energy was heavy with loss—everyone's was. But the addition of a dragon to our midst certainly wouldn't hurt our chances of getting Bodie safely home.

And who knew, maybe our new pet—er, dragon warrior life partner—would end up holding us together until this whole Nott nightmare was behind us, once and for all.

****

After we picked poor Milkir's jaw up off the ground, we ushered him back down the mountain and said our goodbyes. I lingered longer than necessary, watching the Liv pulse in my fingertips as I patted Scarlet. I'd never have admitted it, but I was reluctant to leave my dragon. She was my very first pet and the first warrior life partner I'd ever had. Plus, we had this cool glowy, blue bond between us. Leaving all that behind to continue on what seemed like an impossible quest was a tough pill to swallow.

"Pepper?" Tore called out. "You coming?"

"You can call the Bifrost," I confirmed. "Bodie needs us."

"Heimdall!" Tore shouted into the sky.

While my boyfriend summoned our ride, I turned back to my dragon. "I'll be back soon," I promised, tapping the golden horn at my waist. "And I'll call you if I need you before then."

With one final nuzzle, Scarlet spread her wings and took to the sky, her crimson form momentarily blocking the heat of the sun before disappearing from view. We'd unwittingly shared an experience—the darkness had nearly taken me on Jotunheim, and it had tried to take Scarlet today. We were both survivors. And that bonded us every bit as much as the Liv.

After a beat, a kaleidoscope of colors shot down from the sky, illuminating the little clearing with the shades of the Bifrost. My protectors hurried to step inside its light, leaving Milkir outside the circle.

"Allie. Let's get a move on." Johann waved me forward.

I crossed the grassy space and took Milkir's hands in mine. It pained me to know that we were leaving him behind to bury his brother, but I knew I'd done everything I could to expedite his healing. "Thank you for looking after Scarlet," I told the dwarf. "I'm sorry we couldn't save your brother, too."

Milkir squeezed my hands. "Thank you honoring dragon bond," he said. "I take care of her. Now you save friend."

"I will," I vowed. I meant it. I wouldn't give up until Bodie was returned safely to us.

"We need to go," Tore warned.

"On it." I gave Milkir one final nod and darted into the rainbow to tuck myself against Tore's side. With a sigh, I looked up at the faces of my three protectors. *Three.* My throat pinched with barely-contained grief. The boys were holding it together, and so would I.

"Let's bring Bodie home," Tore growled. "Heimdall, take us to Asgard."

"Asgard?" I asked. "I thought we needed to strategize?"

"We do." Tore stared straight ahead. "Now, Heimdall," he commanded.

The rainbow vibrated, and with a jolt we were sucked in the air, shot through the sky, and deposited in front of the last place I'd ever thought I'd be.

****

The Bifrost ejected us onto a large, glass walkway. It was easily twenty feet wide, ten times as many feet long, and it led to a structure that was altogether unfamiliar. Once I got my bearings, and was fairly confident that I wasn't going to throw up, I turned to Tore.

"What's going on?" I asked.

He threaded his fingers through mine. "I need to do what's best for Bodie."

My favorite protector didn't say any more, just stared straight ahead, pressing his lips together into a thin line. He was obviously wrestling with something he didn't feel like talking about. *Fine.* Instead of pushing the issue, I gave his hand a squeeze. *Got your back, boyfriend. With whatever this is.*

Mack placed a supportive hand on Tore's back. "Are you sure? You haven't seen him in years."

Tore clenched his jaw. "Bodie's worth it. And nobody does revenge better than my father."

A garbled squeak escaped my throat as I realized where we were and what we were about to do.

"I'm meeting your dad." I gave myself a mental facepalm. My clothes were covered in dirt and dragon blood; my hair was a rat's nest, and I was exhausted beyond belief. *Please, Universe, let a coffee-wielding fairy godmother magically appear. Right now. Okay . . . now?*

Sadly, no fairy godmothers were forthcoming. So, I sucked it up like the big girl that I was and changed my tone. "I'm meeting your dad," I repeated, this time with slightly less dread. Then, because I couldn't help myself, I muttered, "Looking like this."

Tore whipped his head around in my direction. "My father's opinion doesn't matter to me. Besides, you look like a warrior. I could do no better."

Aw. My heart melted just a little bit as I hurriedly wove my hair into a knotted braid.

Without another word, Tore marched forward. Mack, Johann, and I followed him across the walkway toward a magnificent home made almost entirely of glass. It stood three stories tall, with multiple chimneys protruding from its arched roof. The structure was surrounded by enough foliage to sustain a municipal garden and framed by a series of silver-leafed oak trees. It would have been the kind of place I dreamed of vacationing to, if it didn't belong to the man who'd stolen the light from my boyfriend's life—Tore's words, not mine.

When we reached the end of the walkway, Johann turned to Tore. "Do you want us to go in or give you privacy?"

"I'd like you guys in there," Tore mumbled. My heart went out to him. Either his ego had finally shrunk to a healthy size, or he was *really* uncomfortable about seeing his father.

Mack and Johann stepped forward. Their unwavering loyalty brought a lump to my throat. As crazy as my life had become, I counted myself majorly lucky to know these guys. They were a family in the very best sense of the word. And I was blessed to get to be a part of it.

Even if it did mean I was about to be face-to-face with the God of Revenge.

"Let's get this over with." Tore raised his fist and banged on the oversized glass door. I stepped closer to his side, burying my anxiety to lend what support I could.

"*Skit.* It's her," Johann grumbled. I shot him a curious stare, and he jutted his chin at the front door. Through the glass, I made out the silhouette of a model-thin woman. The lights of the hallway hit her body as she came closer, and my eyebrows shot up as I took in her six-foot frame. The woman was gorgeous, with raven black hair, big, green doe-eyes, and boobs not at all proportionate to her underfed waist. She wore a sheer dress over her red bikini, and her three-inch heels perfectly matched her bathing suit. And though she looked like she was in her mid-thirties, her abs were *way* more chiseled than mine would ever be.

She must have been on Mack's über-chicken diet, too.

"Who is that?" I whispered.

"Tiri. Just one of my father's mistresses." Tore didn't bother to whisper.

"How many does he have?" *And do they* all *look like that?*

"Too many." Tore shrugged.

By then, Tiri had reached the door. She peered through the glass, her crimson lips forming a pert circle as she registered the four of us standing on the other side. She fumbled with the handle before yanking the door open.

"Well, well, well. Look who's gracing us with his presence. You must need something from your father." Tiri placed one hand on her waist and jutted out her hip.

"Where's Revenge?" Tore growled.

"Vidar is in the swimming pool. Follow me." Tiri sidestepped the open door, turning on one high-heeled foot to sashay across the white marble floor. Her raven waves swung back and forth with each fluid step, and her hips moved with practiced precision. If the Norse pantheon boasted a Goddess of Seduction, odds were high this girl had the gig. And she had a thing with Tore's dad?

We made our way through the all-white entry, past what must have been hundreds of thousands of dollars of ornate, ivory-hued decor. The entire house was sterile and modern; beautiful, but far from comfortable. We rounded the corner to another sterile room. It must have been a living space, because in addition to the white-on-white decorating scheme, it boasted a cream-colored couch, an oversized ottoman, and an enormous, black dog snoring belly up in his white, fleecy dog bed.

Revenge had a pet?

"Killer!" Tore shouted. The dog's eyes snapped open, and he spun onto his stomach so quickly, he flopped right out of his dog bed.

Killer?

The dog pushed himself onto all fours and whipped his head around to look at Tore. He craned his neck back to give a long howl before scraping his claws on the marble floor. Once he had enough traction, he took off at a run, charging straight at us.

Fear clenched my heart like a vise, and in an act of straight-up self-preservation, I dropped Tore's hand and scurried behind Mack. Tore threw out his arms just before Killer leapt into the air. The demigod nearly fell over beneath two hundred plus pounds of dog, but instead of groaning, Tore laughed heartily. Killer howled again before burying his face in Tore's neck and sniffling hard.

"Aw," Mack sighed. I cautiously poked my head around his arm and looked up to see tears in the lumberjack's eyes.

"He missed you," Tiri surmised.

Tore glared at her. "Of course, he did. He's *my* dog."

Tiri rolled her eyes, then turned and sauntered toward the back of the house. "I'll go get your father."

"You do that," Tore muttered. He set Killer down, and the dog scampered in a circle, yipping and howling. He seemed friendly enough . . . but he also seemed enthusiastic enough to take me down in one well-intentioned leap.

"Mack, prop me up," I instructed. My friend chuckled as I stepped in front of him and held out my hand. "Hey there, uh, Killer."

The dog approached tentatively, his shoulder level with my hip as he sniffed my hand. No doubt he caught a hefty whiff of dragon along with a solid dose of Tore. The familiar smell must have won him over, because he plopped on the ground, nearly crushing my feet as he rolled over to expose his belly. I was no dog expert, but I was pretty sure this meant, "Welcome to the family."

One Vidarsson down, one to go.

I bent down to oblige Killer with a friendly pat. Mack and Johann knelt beside me, so the three of us were rubbing Killer's enormous belly when heavy footsteps stormed into the room. Either Tiri had put on some major pounds, or I was about to meet the God of Revenge. *Oh, Lord. Here goes nothing.*

I tilted my head up, then up some more. Tore's dad was *huge.* He must have been close to seven feet tall, and his biceps were easily as big as Killer's head. He'd clearly just come from the pool—the towel draped over his broad shoulders caught the droplets of water that fell from his shaggy, black hair. More drops streamed down his bare torso, trailing the line of tribal-looking chest tattoos. The ink extended down Vidar's chest, disappearing beneath the waist of his white swim trunks. Clearly the guy had a color-theme going.

"Son." Vidar's ice-blue eyes cut right into Tore. The entire room descended into awkward silence.

"I'm not your son. You denounced me, remember?" Tore's cold glare was the mirror image of his father's. They glowered at each other while Tiri sauntered over to offer Vidar another towel. Mack, Johann, and I stood up, ready to fight or flee, depending on Tore's next move.

"You're still upset about that? Get over it, boy." Vidar snatched the towel from Tiri and ran it over his dripping hair. "Who's the girl?"

I swallowed hard and had to lean on Mack as I tried not to choke to death on my own saliva. *Awesome first impression, Allie. Nailed it.*

"Uh, hi." I coughed. "I'm Allie. Eir's daughter."

My awkward hacking didn't exactly scream *demigod*.

"Allie is my girlfriend." Tore stepped back to take my hand. My stomach did a tiny leap at the way he introduced me, but Vidar's expression was cold. No smile; no nothing. *Huh.* It wasn't looking like I'd have a spot on the family Christmas card come December.

"You know Revenge and a healer didn't work before," Vidar said drily.

Beside me, Mack gave a soft growl. Killer bared his teeth at the sound. *Crap.*

Tore dropped my hand and stormed toward his father. "Don't. Ever. Speak. Of. My. Mother. Again." His hands were clenched, and his body shook with rage. My breath caught as his shield dropped, exposing his energy signature. Red and black threads of anger and pain wove around his heart. The density of loss and trauma were imprinted in his gut. But the rest of Tore's energy was blue—nearly the same shade as the Liv. Was he like me on the inside, too?

Before I could delve deeper, Tore's shield snapped back into place. He and his father were locked in the mother of all staredowns, and if the clenched jaws and bulging biceps were any indication, this was going to end in a bigtime fight. Somebody needed to intervene.

And I doubted Tiri was up to the job.

I pulled my shoulders back and projected a confidence I *so* did not feel. "Our friend Bodie was pushed into a dark portal on Nidavellir. We think Nott has him, and we need your help getting him back."

Revenge didn't take his gaze off Tore. "Is that right, son? You need my help?"

I sent all the positive energy I could to Tore, because I knew it would take a hell of a lot of pride-swallowing for him to answer that question.

The vein over Tore's jaw pulsed, and I could practically hear his teeth grinding together. "Yes," he gritted out. "I need your help."

Vidar placed a hand on Tore's shoulder with a grin. "That wasn't so hard, was it?"

Tore spun around. My eyes widened at the murderous look on his face.

Vidar opened his arms. "I'm currently engaged in an operation for the Alfödr. You may have heard rumors of a potential spy in Asgard. At the moment, my plate is full spearheading that investigation."

My stomach dropped.

"So, you won't help," Tore said in a flat voice.

Vidar shook his head. "I didn't say that. I can't personally see to the mission but I can spare a few of my warriors to look into your situation. I'll have them report to you in . . ." he glanced at the clock over the fireplace. "Four hours should do it."

Tore nodded. "Thank you." His tone was more like, 'screw you,' but he was trying. Since nobody had thrown any punches *and* Vidar had agreed to help us find Bodie, I was calling this visit a win.

Vidar stepped forward and clapped Tore on the back. "I knew you would come around. It's about time you learned the family business."

Tore shrugged him off. "I'm not . . . never mind. I'm taking my dog."

"Fine." Vidar shrugged.

"Fine," Tore retorted.

Silence again descended on the living room. Mack broke it with a deep, Namaste bow. "*Takk*, Sir. We should get back and prepare things on our end."

Vidar shot an icy glare at Tore's back. But his expression softened when he said, "You are welcome to return, anytime."

Tore snorted. He took Killer by the collar and guided him out of Vidar's house. Johann followed, with Mack and me bringing up the rear.

"Nice to meet you both," I said awkwardly. Tiri ignored me, but Vidar gave a tight nod. We closed the door behind us, and I shuddered. Now I knew why my favorite protector was so complicated. *Yikes. Talk about daddy issues.*

Once we reached the end of the glass walkway, I looked down at Killer. "Can dogs travel on the Bifrost?"

"The force could harm a Midgardian canine," Tore said. "But Asgardian ones are a lot stronger."

"I gathered." I'd seen Killer nearly take Tore down with a friendly jump.

Tore grinned. "I think you're going to find that Killer's a different breed than the kinds of dogs you're used to."

"Yeah, a larger, stronger, more drool-prone breed." Mack frowned. "Are you really planning on keeping him at the safe house?"

"You got a problem with that?" Tore raised an eyebrow at our neat-freak friend.

"We can figure out the pet arrangements later," Johann chimed in. "Between Allie's dragon and Tore's dog, we're going to have a lot of adjustments to make. But right now, Bodie is our priority. That's why we came here. Now move."

We all sobered at Johann's reminder. Tore called for the Bifrost, and without another word, we stepped into the rainbow. Vidar's warriors wouldn't be able to help us for another few hours, which meant we needed to have an airtight plan in place by the time they arrived. Who knew what Nott could do to Bodie in that time? And who knew what kind of army she was amassing on her end? Not that any of that mattered. We were going to bring our friend home.

No matter what it cost us.

CHAPTER SEVEN

BACK IN CANADA, WE wasted no time getting to work on an extraction plan. Operation Breakout Bodie would require total focus, which meant recovering Gud Morder's missing pieces had to wait. We hunkered down in the living room to map out our strategy. Johann threw some logs in the fireplace, and Killer made himself at home in front of the flames. The big, black dog chewed contentedly on a corner of the area rug, and it was a testament to Mack's love for Tore that he spoke nothing of the travesty. But I did notice an unprecedented twitch in the light elf's jaw. And he disappeared for a solid minute, returning in a hurry to deposit an enormous tree branch in front of the canine. Killer shifted his oral focus to the branch, eliciting a relieved sigh from my tidy protector. Once Killer's teeth were redirected, Mack stood at attention beside the window, arms folded behind his back and eyes staring at the rug-chewer. I had no doubt that he intended to steam clean the carpet the second he got the chance.

Johann and I took seats on the floor beside Killer. I buried my fingertips in the dog's fur, taking comfort in the happy grunts coming from our oversized pet, while Tore paced angrily around the couch.

"Listen up," Tore barked. His heels hit the hardwood floor with more force than I was accustomed to. "Vidar's team won't report in for three and a half hours, and I have no intention of sitting on my butt until then. Mack, do a quick inquiry into the conditions in Vanaheim."

"Vanaheim?" Johann looked up.

"*Ja.* I thought we could pay your dads a visit. Hjalmar was stationed in Muspelheim on his last tour, right?" Tore didn't stop pacing.

"He was," Johann confirmed. "You think he can give us information Vidar can't?"

"I think your father can give us perspective that Vidar *won't*," Tore corrected. "I don't trust Revenge to look after anything beyond his own agenda. For all I know, he'll feed his intel team information that pushes Asgard straight into war with the fire giants. I want to extract Bodie safely, but I want to make sure we cause as little damage as possible doing it."

"Fair enough." Johann pushed himself up. "Do you want me to call my dads and let them know we're coming?"

"Yes," Tore confirmed. Johann nodded as he walked into the hall. His boots pounded on the stairs as he jogged up to his room and, I guessed, his phone. A while back, I'd asked Mack how the guys made off-realm calls. Apparently, they'd incorporated a chip developed by some Asgardian super-brain into standard issue smartphones, extending the device range to include the whole entire cosmos. Guess there really was an app for everything.

"Good." Tore nodded. "Johann will contact his fathers. Hjalmar should be able to give us good intel."

My fingers dug deeper into Killer's fur. Today was a big day for meeting my protectors' parents. I hoped Tore was going to let me shower before we took off again. Maybe put on blood-free clothes while I was at it. We'd had so much going on, I hadn't had time to process the fact that Bodie was gone, I had a new piece of Gud Morder, and now I was responsible for keeping a dragon's soul from dying. *Yeesh.*

"Mack." Tore kept pacing. "As part of your inquiry, confirm there are no active hostilities in Vanaheim. Then prepare our travel weapons." Tore ripped his beanie off his head and shoved it into his back pocket.

"On it." Mack gave Killer one more wary look, before stalking into the hallway and heading for his room.

"What do I do?" I asked quietly.

Tore ran his hands over the snarled mess of his hair. "You just try to keep me sane, Allie."

My heart melted. *Oh, Tore.* Without a word, I tucked my feet beneath me and stood before crossing the living room to wrap my arms around my boyfriend. Tore's torso tensed before he relaxed into my embrace. With a heavy exhale, he pulled me tight against his chest and rested his chin on the top of my head.

"This is my fault," he rumbled. His chin moved against my scalp as he spoke.

"No, it's my fault," I corrected. "Bodie was trying to save me."

"*Ja*, but I'm the one who left him up there to protect you. That was my job—not his. I should have sent him down after Mack and Johann." Tore's chest shuddered. His wave of remorse was so fierce, it washed over me, too.

"You're *all* my protectors. You took an oath to the Alfödr, remember? Bodie knew what he was signing on for." My thumbs made circles at the small of Tore's back. "But we'll get him back. I promise, we will. His energy's too powerful to be overtaken by anyone—even Nott."

"Gods, I hope you're right." Tore's lips brushed against my hair.

"I'm glad I got to meet your dad today," I offered.

"I'm not," Tore growled. "My dad's a monster. I wouldn't have gone to him if I'd had any other option. But I knew he'd help us. He's wanted to take down Nott for a long time."

"Why? What did Nott do to him? Try to kill his mistress or something?" The thought of the big-boobed, raven-haired chick set my teeth on edge. She'd treated Tore like his mere existence was a mighty burden on her otherwise perfect life.

"Yes," Tore replied.

Oh.

He didn't say any more. Since I knew he was still teetering on the edge of losing it, I changed the subject. "And now we have a dog. Big day for pets, around here."

From his place beside the fire, Killer let out a contented chuff.

"Right, the dog." Tore pulled away from me to study Killer. "I'd better call someone to watch him while we're gone. He'll break right out of the training complex, and Mack would probably kill me if I left him in the house, huh?"

"I think you're pushing Mack's inner clean-freak pretty far today. Can you imagine what will happen when we find a way to bring home the dragon? Poor guy might actually have a heart attack."

"We're going to need a bigger safe house." One corner of Tore's mouth tugged up in a smile, and I gave myself an internal high five. Mission accomplished.

"Who are you going to get to babysit Killer, anyway?" I asked. "I'm pretty sure we can't bring him to a kennel. He'd scare the other dogs." Or maybe just eat them.

Tore kissed me lightly, then walked toward the stairs. "I'm going to ask Greta to come watch him for a few hours. She needs to know what's happened to Bodie anyway, and I'd rather she heard it directly from me."

Oh, God. "You want me to be with you while you tell her?"

"No." Tore's long hair brushed against his shoulders as he shook his head. "Bodie's under my command; it's my job to make these calls."

"Just because it's our job doesn't mean you have to do it alone," I said gently.

"I know that." Tore looked back over his shoulder. "I'd have turned back into the head case

Revenge wants me to be if you hadn't been there to ground me today. You make me a better man, Allie Rydell."

My insides promptly melted into a warm, gooey mush. *Could he be any sweeter?*

Without another word, Tore turned back around and resumed climbing the stairs, leaving me to stare at his absolutely spectacular butt as his words spun around inside my head. Who'd have ever guessed the jerk I pepper sprayed on campus would win my heart?

"Wait," I called feebly after him. "What do you need me to do?"

He tilted his head to wink over his shoulder. "Go take a shower. I know you want to wash all that blood out of your hair. And knowing you're naked and wet somewhere in this house will make getting through my next few minutes a hell of a lot more bearable."

All of the blood that didn't immediately rush to my cheeks headed straight south, creating a slow burn that made me *very* glad Tore had turned back around. *Holy hell. Did he really just say that?* By the time Tore made it to the top of the stairs and rounded the corner, I needed that shower for reasons that exceeded dragon blood removal.

I retreated to my room and got to work removing the physical evidence of my day. When my skin and hair were scrubbed free of blood and my heartbeat had returned to a somewhat normal rate, I put on a clean tank top and a fresh pair of pants, tied my hair into a tight braid, and brushed on some light makeup. As I opened the door that led from my bathroom to my bedroom, the massive blond figure holding court on the edge of my bed made me jump. Tore kept himself perfectly still with his head tilted down to study the piece of paper he clutched in his hands. My heart skyrocketed at the sight of his wet hair, low-slung cargos, and tight t-shirt. He'd cleaned up, too. And he looked *really good.*

"Hey." I breathed, trying not to die at the knowledge that Tore Vidarsson was sitting on my bed. Ninety more degrees and he'd be lying down. And then I could—*no, Allie. Not the time. Focus.*

Tore looked at me with a sexy lopsided grin. "You know it took every ounce of control I possess to not pick that lock and join you in the shower."

Screw focus. Jump him now. Right now.

I wiped my suddenly sweaty palms on my jeans and took slow steps across the room. "The door wasn't locked."

Tore's Adam's apple rose and fell. His eyes deepened a shade as he raked his bottom lip between his teeth. He set the paper on the bed and shifted his body to face me. *Seriously? Now?* His timing couldn't have been worse. Our friend desperately needed our help, and our rainbow-ride was due to drop in at any minute. But good God, Tore was a beautiful distraction—one my overworked brain and gutted heart desperately needed to focus on to keep from going insane. I stepped determinedly forward, completely intending to distract myself to the full extent our time constraints would allow. But as I reached the edge of the bed, my eyes fell to the piece of paper. It wasn't a paper at all; it was a photograph. My jump-Tore plan came to a screeching halt as I took in the familiar-looking blonde woman on the page.

"Tore?" I asked, all dirty thoughts wiped totally clean. "Is that . . ."

He followed my sight line to the picture. When he spoke, his voice shook a little. "It's my mom."

Oh. My. God.

I plopped onto the edge of the bed next to him, partly because my knees were weak and partly because I had no idea what to say. *Holy hell. He's going to talk about his mom?* Gratitude and anxiety wrestled for control over my heart. I didn't want to screw this up.

"I figured after meeting my epic jerk of a dad and his play thing, I needed to tell you about the amazing woman who raised me and put up with Vidar's crap."

My heart hammered so hard, dizziness threatened to overcome me. This was the moment I'd been waiting for, the moment where Tore finally trusted me enough to open up to me. With one finger, I carefully touched the edge of the photo. The similarities between Tore and the woman standing near a waterfall were striking. He had his mother's blonde hair and radiant smile. And the dimple in his left cheek was a slightly less pronounced version of the one on his mother's right one. I glanced up, and my fourth center warmed at the loving way Tore stared at the photo. It was clear his mother had once been his world—and I was beyond honored that he was showing her to me now.

I stayed quiet, not wanting to spook Tore. Sharing this part of his life with me was a huge step, and I wasn't sure how he wanted to proceed. When Tore continued to stare silently at the picture, I threw out a lifeline.

Dear Universe, Please make Tore say something. I really *don't want to guess wrong here. Xoxo, Allie.*

After a full minute of silence, the universe answered my plea in the most unexpected way. Tore shifted so he looked me square in the eye. Then he took a deep breath and dropped his energy shield.

Holy mother. Tore. Vidarsson. Dropped. His. Energy. Shield.

I tried not to make a big deal out of it, but I couldn't stop my gasp; Tore had caught me by surprise. And now that he was away from his father, his underlying energy was breathtaking. It was a deep magenta with wide streaks of radiant Liv-blue. The resonance of his centers revealed his bravery and his deep capacity for unconditional love. But near his heart, there were hooks of black and brown, emotional injuries that he hadn't yet allowed himself to heal.

I reached out and took one of his hands in both of mine. He met my gaze with one of intense anger. *Whoa.*

"I was an unplanned pregnancy." He spat out the words. "My father met my mother, and after a few weeks of dating they, you know. Then he bailed on her for the next thing."

I could see now why he looked so upset.

"Demigods aren't easy to create," he continued. "A titled god and an untitled god are rarely able to produce offspring. But when they do, the baby is treasured by the realm. My father had always wanted an heir, and when my mom found out she was pregnant, she tracked my dad down and shared the big news. He was surprised, but also happy. His ego wanted a demigod of revenge. My mom was fully prepared to raise me herself, but my father said he wanted to marry her and raise their child together. I imagine he was genuinely trying to do the right thing. My mom, of course, was thrilled—she'd been in love with my father since their first date."

I stroked Tore's hand, unable to take my eyes off the dark brown energy hooks in his heart. The more he talked, the bigger they grew.

"So, they were married. And I was born. And instead of doing the right thing and being a decent husband," Tore's nostrils flared, "or at the very least, just bailing on her so she could find someone else, he screwed around on her. He cheated, verbally and emotionally abused her, and made her life a living Hel. She took it because she loved me, and she wanted me to have a father that was around."

"I'm so sorry." I told him, unable to stop the tears that had formed in my eyes.

He shrugged. "One night in high school, when I was away on a camping trip . . ." His voice trembled, and he paused to take a breath. "My dad had a lot of enemies; he knew that. Instead of staying at home to protect my mother while I was gone, he was off with one of his side whores. My mother was burned alive in our family home by some dark realm thugs who had beef with Revenge."

I gasped. "No."

Tore clutched the picture so hard that his knuckles turned white. "He let me stay on my trip for the rest of the week, didn't come to tell me.

What kind of prick does that? I came back to a new house; no mother, no funeral, nothing."

Tears streamed freely down my face. I mopped them away with one hand. "I can't imagine."

"I ran away after that, stayed with Bodie for a bit, spent some time with Johann and his dads. Mack's parents even took me in for a while—the Alfödr partnered Mack and me up when we enlisted, probably thought Mack could meditate me out of my issues." Tore sighed. "I haven't been home since then. Well, until today."

I leaned forward to press my forehead against Tore's. "I wish I could have met your mom."

He smiled. "She would have loved you. That's part of why I pushed you away for so long. I never wanted to care about someone, then fail them, again."

"What do you mean?" I asked.

"I knew Revenge had enemies, and I knew my mom could be their target. But I went on that camping trip because I stupidly believed my father was god enough to protect his family. He wasn't. I should have known that. And that puts her death on my shoulders. I should have protected my mother, Allie. But I *will* protect you. Still, fear haunts me. What if I'm not around and something happens to you? Gods, I would die if—"

I shut him up with a kiss, pressing my lips hard against his. He responded immediately, setting the photo down and framing my waist with his hands. Shifting positions, he lifted me backward onto the bed, then swung one leg over mine to straddle me. "Allie," he murmured, before sliding his hands up the back of my shirt and crushing his mouth against mine again. I sighed as the weight of his torso shifted against me, pushing me down onto the mattress. When my back was nestled deep in the plushy comforter, Tore lowered himself on top of me. The full length of his body pressed against mine, from the rock-hard muscles of his pecs to the thick trunks of his thighs.

Oh. My. God. Please. Yes.

I reached up to snake my hands inside Tore's shirt, feeling the corded muscles of his back while I pulled him closer to me. He moved his tongue against mine before he shifted again, sending a tremor rocking all the way through my body. Holy hell, if this was what kissing Tore fully-clothed was like, I couldn't *wait* to get him naked. *Naked . . . the* thought sent another tremor through me, and if we hadn't been minutes away from catching a Bifrost out of Vancouver, I'd have ripped his shirt off right then. Instead, I exercised tremendous restraint and moved my hands up to cup his cheeks. I withdrew my tongue and planted a chaste kiss on his bottom lip. He raised his head and looked down at me through hooded eyes.

"Too fast?" he panted.

"Not fast enough," I countered. "But I'm going to need a *lot* more time than we've got right now. And besides, I have a question."

Tore groaned and rolled onto his back beside me. He ran his fingers through his disheveled hair. "Shoot."

"Well." I rolled onto my stomach and rested my forearms on his chest. "You said fear was part of why you pushed me away. What's the other part?"

Tore reached up to tuck an errant strand behind my ear. "Really? I have to remind you of the assault you committed at our first meeting?"

Embarrassment coursed through my energy centers, but I shirked it off with a playful eye roll. "Meeting? I would hardly call stalking me in the park a meeting. Let it go."

One corner of his mouth pulled up in a lazy smirk. "Kiss me like that again, and I'll let it go."

"Mmm. Maybe I will," I teased.

Tore framed my waist with his hands again and pulled me on top of him in one quick move. *Yes, please.* My lips met his, and for an endless moment I gave myself over to the feeling of his mouth on mine, his hands on my butt, and the way his thick biceps flexed beneath my fingertips.

Much too quickly, Tore rolled so we lay side by side. He withdrew his kiss, and I nearly face-planted in my desire to maintain full lip contact. *Dang it.* As I recovered, he fixed his ice-blue eyes on me and reached up to gently hold both sides of my face.

"Allie Rydell, I'm in love with you," he murmured.

I stopped breathing. *Super-hot demi-god say what?*

Tore raised one eyebrow. "You okay?"

"You love me?" I whispered.

"More than I can possibly tell you." He stroked my cheek with one thumb, sending a surge of warmth through my body.

"Good," I murmured. "Because I love you, too." Then I grinned like an idiot.

At the edge of my vision, the hooks in Tore's heart lightened to a pale brown. As I glanced down to examine the change, a flash of light burst through my bedroom window. A prism of colors filled the room as the Bifrost dropped in, and Tore quickly brought his shield back down. He pushed himself up on one elbow and removed his hand from my cheek to squeeze my butt.

"What do you think? Can I get a raincheck on this make out session?" Tore asked.

Laughter bubbled from deep in my chest. "Only if you're good."

"Oh, Pepper." Tore swung his legs over the edge of the bed and stood up. "I'm *very* good. Hope you can handle me."

I sat up and quickly re-braided my hair. "I hope *you* can handle *me,* Protector."

A low growl built in Tore's throat. "Gods, you're sexy." He picked up my armor from the chair in the corner of my room and held it out. He must have brought it downstairs with him when I was in the shower. "You need help putting this on?"

"Sure." I slid my arm into the shoulder piece and turned so Tore could strap me into it. Then I slid the cuff over my wrist and retrieved the photo of Tore's mom from where it had been abandoned on the edge of the bed. *Oops.* "Thank you for sharing her with me." I smiled at the photo before handing it to Tore.

"Thank *you*, Allie. For letting me see I don't have to be alone."

My heart absolutely melted.

"Of course," I whispered.

Tore crossed to the door and pulled it open. "Bifrost's down, which means Greta will be here any minute. I'm going to run this picture upstairs and grab a few extra weapons. Meet you on the porch in two?"

"Yup." I watched his beautiful backside exit my bedroom, committing the visual to memory. *Holy mother. What a day.*

Tore had barely disappeared from view when I heard the pounding on the front door. The noise sent poor Killer into a near-apoplectic fit of barking that made the pictures on the wall tremble.

"Down, Killer!" I commanded as I walked into the entryway. He immediately quieted. *Hmm. Cool.* First the dragons, now the dog. Maybe I was becoming an animal whisperer.

Greta flew into my arms the second I wrenched the door open. Tears streamed down her cherubic face, leaving twin wet trails flowing from her emerald eyes. I raised an eyebrow when I looked over her shoulder—Greta had been joined by her shorter doppelganger. The girl's fiery red hair was a few shades darker than Greta's strawberry hue, and she was obviously a few years younger. But other than that, they were nearly identical.

"Greta?" I held her at arm's length to study her heartbroken face. "Are you okay?"

"I can't believe Nott took Bodie." She wiped her tears on her sleeve.

"I know," I whispered. "I'm so sorry."

Footsteps on the stairs pulled my attention away from my friend. Tore jogged toward us wearing more weapons than a ninja.

"*Hei*, Greta. Hey, Mel—what are you doing here?" Tore raised a hand to greet the teenager on the porch.

She stepped inside, gesturing to Killer. "Dog watching, I guess."

Tore and I furrowed our brows in unison. Greta crossed her arms at our disapproving expressions. "I'm going with you guys, whether you like it or not," she declared.

Tore groaned. "Greta, you're not battle trained. You can help Bodie by staying here and staying safe."

With a glare, Greta pulled her crystal wands from her bag. She raised them over her head and clapped them together, sending a shock wave through the entryway that made Tore and me fall into each other. I managed to right myself, but Tore landed hard on his butt.

"What the Hel!" he scolded.

Greta placed her hands on her hips. "I can take care of myself, Tore Vidarsson, and you know it."

Holy mother, Greta was fierce.

Killer sniffed Tore's hand and gave him a big lick before trotting over to sit beside Mel. Tore sighed as he pushed himself to his feet. "Fine, but if you're going with us, it's *only* as the team healer.

You're going to stay in the back, and you're going to stay out of the way."

"Fine." Greta re-crossed her arms.

Tore looked down at her before adding, "And teach Allie that wand-clap thing."

She mock saluted. "Yes, sir."

Tore turned to me. "Why can't you call me sir?"

I rolled my eyes. "You wish."

"I do," he agreed.

The slam of the back door was followed by the clomp of heavy footsteps. A moment later, a snow-covered Johan and Mack emerged from the kitchen, their arms laden with weapons.

"*Hei*, Greta. Mel." The guys deposited their weapons in the hallway before giving Greta and her sister hugs.

"What are you doing here, Mel?" Johann asked.

"Greta's going with you guys, and she says I have to watch the dog." Mel shrugged.

Mack nodded and pulled Mel aside. "Take Killer outside to urinate every hour. If he has an accident, use the baking soda cleaning mixture in the blue bowl on the kitchen counter. It should work on the area rugs without damaging their coloring."

Mel raised one eyebrow. "O-kay."

"Don't let him chew on anything," Mack continued. "We'll get dog toys when we return, but for now, sticks will have to do. I've left a pile outside of the back door. Use the bigger ones first; they'll take him longer to work through."

Mel laughed. "We'll be fine. My healing tutor is coming by later, so between the two of us, we'll manage to keep the dog in check."

Mack patted her shoulder, the tension never leaving his face. I tried to telepath him serene thoughts, but he didn't look any less stressed. I made a mental note to work on my clairvoyance skills with Greta, too.

"Okay, we'll be back in a few hours." Tore ran his hands through his hair. "Hopefully, before Revenge's team gets here and we have to leave for Muspelheim."

While I nodded my head, I wondered if anyone else's stomach was in knots. *No? Just mine?*

"My dads are ready for us," Johann chimed in. "Let's head out before Garrett bakes any more welcome-home pastries. Hjalmar's back on his paleo diet, and it drives him nuts when there's an excess of sweets around the *hus.*"

"Uh, I'm happy to relieve your *hus* of any and all sweets," I volunteered.

"Me too," Greta agreed. "In the name of saving your dads a fight, of course."

"Right," Johann chuckled. "Well, shall we head out?"

"Grab your weapons, and let's move," Tore ordered. We gathered around the pile of swords, daggers, and arrows and selected our favorite pieces. Tore helped me re-adjust the straps on my armor before he opened the front door. Johann, Greta, and I filed through, but our light elf friend lingered behind. "Mack, come *on*," Tore urged.

"Coming," Mack grumbled. He emerged backward onto the porch, still calling out instructions about the proper use of his homemade cleaning solution. If this whole protector thing didn't work out, Mack definitely had a future in home maintenance.

"Goodbye, Mack," Mel replied with a laugh. "See you guys in a few hours."

Tore closed the door behind him before jogging to the clearing. "You know the drill. We get in, get our intel, and get back here. The weapons are just precautionary; I don't anticipate encountering any hostiles in Vanaheim. Recovering Bodie is our priority; everything else will have to wait."

"Agreed," I voiced, and the rest of our group nodded.

"Good." Tore looked to the clouds. "Heimdall," he shouted. "Open the Bifrost!"

And with that, the rainbow bridge shot down from the sky, sucking us upward and bringing us one step closer to getting our friend back.

CHAPTER EIGHT

"GOD, I HATE THE BIFROST." I buried my face in Tore's chest while the realm of Vanaheim circled my head in a dizzying blur. Green and white swirls gave way to the black of Tore's t-shirt, and I regained my footing by focusing on the sensation of my boyfriend's strong pecs pressed against my cheek. *Mmm. Much better.*

"You okay?" Tore rubbed his hand along my back.

"Never better," I muttered. The nightmare that was inter-realm travel was nothing in comparison to whatever horrors Bodie was surely experiencing. And the longer it took me to recover from my travel sickness, the longer it would take us to rescue our friend. With resolve, I commenced the deep yogic breaths Mack had taught me to use in order to cope with Bifrost travel. *In through the nose, out through the mouth. Drop my grounding anchor. Good. Now, let's hurry up and do this so we can save Bodie.*

With my equilibrium restored, I raised my head to catch my first stationary view of Vanaheim. The greens and whites that had whirled past my eyes turned out to be forest and snow. My friends and I stood ankle deep in a grass-filled meadow, with moss-wrapped evergreens on one side and snowcapped mountains on the other. A village rested at the foot of the mountains, providing its residents easy access to what looked like miles of pristine powder and epic cornices. *Wow.* I made a mental note to ask Tore to bring me back here for a ski date once we'd recovered Bodie and the Nott nightmare was behind us. Somewhere up there was a trail that needed my name carved into it.

"Everybody ready to move out?" Tore called to the group.

A fast headcount revealed that Greta, Mack, and Johann were huddled in a tight clump beside Tore and me. Mack held his crossbow at eye level, but after turning a quick circle, he strapped it over his shoulder with a nod. "We're clear. Johann, lead the way."

"Aye, aye." Johann mock saluted. "Head to the village, and go straight up the main road. My place is a quarter-mile up the hill."

"I haven't been to your realm in a while, Johann," Greta said. "But isn't the forest normally snowy this time of year?"

I glanced at the emerald moss climbing the evergreens. There wasn't a flake of snow anywhere near the trees.

"I thought so, but I haven't been home in a while, either. Tore's kept us pretty busy the past few years," Johann said.

"Has my training regimen been too taxing for you?" Tore slung an arm around my shoulder.

"Not at all," Johann chuckled. "But Mack's morning mindfulness lectures definitely have been."

"If you don't want to be enlightened, by all means, keep on sleeping in." Mack shrugged.

"Come on." Greta stamped one petite foot. "Bodie is gods knows where, and he needs our help. Move it."

I liked the healer's style.

The boys jumped to action, marching forward in a protective cluster around Greta and me. We reached the edge of the meadow, then headed into town. Johann's village was a hub of activity. Despite the cool temperature, residents were out in full force for Vanaheim's version of a farmers' market. Wooden carts lined the cobblestone streets, their beams draped with animal pelts and freshly-slaughtered poultry. *Ew.* Other stands held row upon row of exotic-looking fruits and vegetables—glittery red spheres that sparkled in the sunlight, deep green leaves big enough to be a dinosaur's version of kale, and a spiky purple orb that may have been delicious but looked way too much like Mack's mace for me to want to eat it. As we walked through town, shoppers called out to each other in greeting, and more than a handful enveloped Johann in warm hugs.

We passed another fruit cart, and Johann stopped to grin at a rotund woman clad in a white apron. "Mrs. Maraki," he said. "It's been too long."

My friends and I clustered behind Johann as Mrs. Maraki clapped his back joyfully. The tassels of her fur-lined hat bounced as she released him from her hold. "Oh, Hannie, welcome home! Your fathers will be so happy to see you!"

"They'd better be." Johann took a woven bag from the pile at her stand and tucked a dozen spiky purple orbs into it. "It's early in the season for pirysans, isn't it? I'm not used to seeing those at market for another month or two."

"It is." Mrs. Maraki shook her head. "The weather's been off this year. The snow has already melted from the forest."

Beside me, Greta raised one eyebrow. "Thought so," she muttered.

Johann turned his head to the trees beyond the meadow where we'd dropped in. He grimaced. "We noticed that."

"Our crops are still fertile, thank the gods, but they produce on different schedules now, unpredictable schedules. The effects of the Night War are taking hold on Vanaheim." Mrs. Maraki frowned. "Alfheim and Nidavellir will be next. And then Asgard."

I shot Tore an anxious look. My gut clenched at his tight nod.

"We won't let it get to that," Mack chimed in. "You have my word."

"Why, Mack Medisjon, while I live and breathe." Mrs. Maraki stepped forward and wrapped her arms around the lumberjack. Clearly, the woman was a hugger.

Mack gently embraced her in return. "*Hei hei*, Mrs. Maraki. It's good to see you again."

Mrs. Maraki stepped back to beam up at Mack. "Did Hannie tell you that pirysan pie recipe you created for me won first prize at the Saint Lucia's bazaar this year? It's going to be featured in the village cookbook."

"I'm glad to hear it." Mack smiled serenely.

"We'll take two dozen with us." Johann tucked the spiky fruits into his bag and drew two gold coins from his pocket. "They're Hjalmar's favorites, so he can eat a few of them raw like the stick in the mud he is. And Garrett can use the remainder to bake more pies for the rest of us."

Mrs. Maraki folded Johann's fingers back over his coins. "Your money's no good here. You just tell Garrett to share some of that pie with me the next time I see him."

"Oh, he will. But I insist." Johann placed his money near the till on the corner of the cart. "*Tusen takk,* Mrs. Maraki."

"You always were such a sweet boy. I'm so happy to see you again, Hannie." Mrs. Maraki pinched Johann's cheeks. His ears turned pink as he led us away from her booth.

"So, *Hannie.*" Greta teased as we walked through town. "Seems like your neighbors are glad you're home."

"Yeah," Johann chuckled. "Mrs. Maraki's farm has kept our fridge stocked for as long as I can remember. Bummer to hear Nott's war is affecting her crops."

"I'll say." Tore frowned as he laced his fingers through mine. "I thought Midgard would have to fall before the other light realms were affected. This ups the stakes."

"Well then," I squeezed Tore's hand, "we'd better get Bodie back and get the rest of Gud Morder rebuilt already. Then we can kill Nott and put an end to this once and for all." Not to mention I was overdue for some mother-daughter bonding time.

"You're sexy when you talk destruction. You know that?" Tore winked, sending a surge of heat through my body. I was overdue for some Tore bonding time, too.

I nudged his arm with my shoulder. "Thanks, Protector."

As we walked through town, we passed a series of two-story, stone residences. Some had balconies from which jubilant neighbors waved a hearty *hei hei* to 'Hannie,' while others had snow-dusted yards, in which children played heated games of tag. It took several minutes to reach the edge of town, but before long our boots trod lightly across the snow-packed trail that led to Johann's parents' house. After a few minutes, we stood in front of a two-story home with large windows, sweeping beams, and a wrap-around porch complete with a swing. A tapestry of wintry blooms added color to the flowerboxes beneath the windows, and a warm energy surrounded the entire structure. From the outside, Johann's home was Swiss-chalet-chic meets down-home charm.

My centers opened up to drink in the love that poured from the structure. Johann's house was absolutely lovely.

"Hannie!" The front door flew open, and a slender girl with olive-hued skin charged across the porch. Her long, black hair flew behind her as she threw herself at Johann.

"Jale!" Johann spun the girl in a circle before depositing her onto the snow. "I missed you, sis!"

"I missed you more," she declared.

"Where's our bro?" Johann asked.

"Jarryd's in Asgard on a training mission." Jale stepped back and placed her hands on her hips. "Garrett's been baking like mad since you called. It's hard on him when you're gone. You could visit more, you know."

"I know." Johann's brown eyes crinkled in a smile. "But then you wouldn't get all the pies when I came home. You're welcome."

Jale slugged Johann in the arm. "You're terrible." She laughed before waving at each of us in turn. "*Hei*, Mack, Tore, Greta. And . . ." She drew out the word as she studied me.

"I'm Allie." I waved.

"Oh! You're Eir's daughter." Jale smiled warmly at me. "I'm Jale, Johann's sister. I hope my brother's been behaving himself while he's been protecting you." She glanced at the dagger at my hip. "Though it looks like you can do just fine protecting yourself."

"I'm trying." I shrugged. "It's a steep learning curve."

"No *skit*," Tore muttered. I elbowed him in the ribs.

"Where's Bodie?" Jale looked behind us. "Did he get caught up in the market?"

My heart clenched at the mention of our missing friend. Introductions were well and good, but we needed to get our intel and get out as soon as possible. There would be plenty of time for catching up later—when I had *four* protectors with me, once again.

Tore frowned. "Your dads didn't tell you? Bodie's been abducted. We're hoping Hjalmar has information that will help us get him back."

"Oh, gods." Jale paled considerably. "I didn't know. Get inside, then. We don't have time for small talk, do we?"

Jale waved us onto the porch, where we dropped our weapons into as neat a pile as possible. Once inside the house, smells of chocolate, fruit pies, and love enveloped us. A plump man with short, blond waves stood smiling in the hallway. He walked toward us, dusting his hands on his red checkered apron as he moved. By the time he reached Johann, his face was lit up in a joyful smile. "Hannie!" he exclaimed. "*Velkommen* home!"

"Dad!" Johann threw his arms around his father, and I tried not to giggle at the sheer number of times I'd heard Johann's nickname today. I was going to have to make major use of it when we got back home.

"Oh, my goodness, look at you." Johann's dad held his son at arm's length. "Oh, dear, you're far too thin." He looked up with a frown. "Tore, you promised you wouldn't work him too hard."

"It's not me." Tore released his grip on my hand to raise his palms. "Mack's got us all on this extreme chicken diet while he tries to bulk Allie up. We're not getting nearly enough dessert on Midgard."

"Allie." Johann's dad turned his warm eyes on me. Despite his concern, they bore the same telltale twinkle as his son's. "You probably don't remember me, but I'm Garrett. It's good to see you again. It's been a very long time."

My head tilted in confusion before a flicker of recognition sparked. It pinged between my head and my heart, then lit up my entire being with its warm memory. "That's right, you knew my mom. Know my mom," I corrected myself.

"You've had a lot to take in, haven't you?" Garrett tutted in concern. "We can catch up over the dessert that Mack has failed to make you."

"Hey," Mack protested. "I feed them."

"Someone has to." Johann shrugged. "Eir's cooking gene skipped Allie."

"Oh, just because she's the girl in the house, she's supposed to cook?" Jale's hands were back on her hips. "Pretty backwards, big brother."

"That's not what I—"

"Is that my son?" A booming voice sounded from above us. I drew my attention away from the heckling siblings to take in the massive man descending the staircase. With his jet-black hair, exotic eyes, and dark features, he was a larger copy of Johann . . . minus my friend's playful demeanor. Johann's second dad was all warrior, from his furrowed brow to his set jaw to his bonus-sized triceps. The man was seriously intimidating. A sudden surge of nerves sent my feet shuffling closer to Tore. I clutched his bicep tight, for once not bothering to appreciate its bulk.

"*Hei,* Dad." Johann grinned and crossed to the foot of the stairs. Larger Johann clapped my friend warmly on the back.

"Son." A radiant expression lit up his hard features, siphoning some of my nerves away. "I'm glad you're home. Although I am sorry for the circumstances that brought you here."

"You and me both," Johann said. "Dad, this is Allie—Eir's daughter. Allie, this is my dad, Hjalmar."

"Uh, hello, sir." I bit down on my bottom lip. I needed Hjalmar to like me. The intensity in his eyes, combined with the massiveness of his shoulders, suggested he could crush me if he didn't. After how things had gone down with Tore's dad, I could use a win.

"Oh, Allie." Hjalmar's expression softened. The warrior disappeared, and a worried father took his place. "It's good to see you again. I'm sorry you've gone through so much on your own." He crossed to me in three large steps and enveloped me in a hug.

Vanaheim was turning out to be the realm of the huggers.

"I wasn't on my own," I mumbled into Hjalmar's chest, infinitely relieved I'd gotten his approval. "Gran was with me for most of it. Then I got these guys."

"Mmm-hmm." Hjalmar released his hold to study me with concerned eyes. "And have my son and his friends been taking proper care of you?"

"They're doing fine," I assured him. No need to mention the near-death-by-dragon experience we'd just had, or the fact that my protectors took daily turns kicking my butt in training. "Though I could do with a little more dessert around the house. Mack's got me on this extreme chicken diet . . ." I was totally using Tore's title for the torture that was my food regimen. Except for that one pizza night, it had been nothing but poultry and bacon for weeks. Not that I was complaining about the bacon.

"Well, you've come to the right place." Hjalmar released me to sling an arm around his husband's shoulders. "Garrett has won our village bake-off three years running. I appreciate his prowess—when I'm not off the sugar, of course."

"You don't have to eliminate it completely, Dad." Jale rolled her eyes. "I've told you repeatedly, reducing consumption by half is more than sufficient to improve your metabolic output."

Johann chuckled. "You know Dad can't do anything by halves."

"Truth," Jale agreed.

"Hush, you two," Garrett waved us down the hall. "The cookies are done, and the pie should be cool. I want to feed you while Hjalmar talks to you about how to get Bodie back. Especially you, Allie. You're too thin."

My cheeks grew warm under Garrett's concerned stare. I wasn't used to this many people worrying about me. "Okay," I murmured.

"Oh, these are for you." Johann offered Hjalmar the bag of fruits as we followed Garrett to the kitchen. "I figured Dad would have baked all the ones in the house, and since I know you're on the paleo . . ." He shrugged.

"Thank you, son." Hjalmar beamed down at Johann. "This is very thoughtful."

"That's me." Johann grinned. "Thoughtful."

Tore snorted beside me. *Oh, Hannie. The things we will tease you about later.*

We filed into the all-white kitchen. Brilliant pendant lights hung over the dessert-laden marble island top, and ivory tiles lined the backsplash of the wall that stretched from sink to stove. Garrett donned twin oven mitts to withdraw another tray of sweets from the oven, and Jale pulled plates from the cupboard.

"We'll eat at the table." Hjalmar took utensils from a drawer and scattered them along the island. "And I'll tell you what I know of Muspelheim. Hopefully something will help you locate Bodie."

From my right, Greta let out a delicate sniff. She'd been quiet since the marketplace, and I sensed that Bodie's absence was hitting her hard. Mack reached over to place his hand atop hers. "We'll bring him home, Greta," he pledged.

"I know we will." Greta drew her shoulders back. "And then we'll put every dark elf that contributed to his abduction into an energetic coma. Or worse."

Jale smiled at Greta. "I've always liked you," she declared.

"And I, you," Greta replied soberly.

Garrett waved us to the island, where we filled plates with heaping amounts of sweets. Hjalmar settled at the table looking slightly discontented with his fruit plate, while the rest of us dug into the awesomeness that was Garrett's baking. When our mouths were filled with the first delicious mouthfuls of puff pastry, Hjalmar put his hands on the table and stared us down.

"I'll give you a full report on Muspelheim. But if that's where Bodie is, he's in big-time trouble. The fire giants want a place in Nott's new Midgard, too. Which means if she's hiding your friend there, he's going to be heavily guarded."

Great.

"How heavily guarded?" I asked.

Hjalmar paused before answering. "Think battalions of fire giants on top of active volcanoes. And possibly a handful of possessed dragons."

Terror shot up my spine, ricocheting back downward in a waterfall of pure fear. "That's pretty guarded," I downplayed.

"*Ja*," Hjalmar agreed. "But I have an idea of where you can start your search. On my last tour there, we captured a hostile who'd been hiding in Maldraul Mountain. It's the only inactive volcano in a ring of actives, and most of Muspelheim believes it still spews lava. But the truth is, it dried up centuries ago."

"So Maldraul's inactive, but the rest of the volcanoes could blow at any minute? And you think we should *start* our search there?" That sealed it. Johann's dad was insane.

"Correct." Hjalmar continued. "We interrogated the hostile we captured, and he gave us a fairly detailed explanation of the caverns within the mountain. They'd make the perfect hiding spot for a night goddess who didn't want to be found."

I leaned over to whisper in Tore's ear. "By 'interrogated,' Hjalmar totally means 'tortured,' doesn't he?" *Insane.*

"Yup." Tore didn't bat an eye. "What's the breakdown on the interior?"

Hjalmar reached behind him to grab the pad of paper and pen that rested on the countertop. Tore and Johann scooted their chairs closer to the warrior while he sketched out a map, but Mack nudged me with his elbow.

"What?" I asked.

The lumberjack jutted his chin at Greta. She was staring morosely into her napkin.

"You need me?" I murmured to Tore. With a subtle head tilt, I directed his attention to Greta.

He took one look at our friend and shook his head. "I'll fill you in later," he whispered.

Turning from Tore, I reached out to take Greta's free hand in my own. "Hey," I whispered. "Can I borrow you in the hallway for a minute?"

"Don't the guys need us here?" she asked.

"Too many cooks in this kitchen. They'll fill us in on the extraction strategy later. Come on." I pushed my chair back and led Greta from the table. When we were away from the recon talk, I pulled her in for a hug. She stiffened before relaxing into my embrace. "You doing okay?"

"No," she admitted. She wrapped her arms around me and held on tight.

"I'm so sorry, Greta," I said. "It's my fault Bodie's gone. He was trying to protect me, and—"

"Stop it. This is Nott's fault. Nobody else's." She pulled away with a frown. "It's just that given everything that's happened to Eir . . . well, I'm nervous."

"Tell me about it." I grimaced. I'd kept a tight lid on my worries because I knew that if I unleashed them, I'd fall to pieces and be of no use to our missing friend—or to the team of protectors who were his only hope of escape. No way was I letting that happen.

"Sorry, Allie. I didn't mean to bring up your mom."

My gut clenched as a fresh wave of sadness washed over me. *Sorry, Mom. We'll break your curse soon, I swear.* But from everything I'd heard of her, my mom was a loyal friend. She'd understand our needing to save Bodie before we found the next piece of Gud Morder. I hoped.

"It's okay." I drew my shoulders back with resolve. "The good news is that Nott needs Bodie alive to use him as bait, so we at least have that going for us. And Hjalmar's information is going to help us track him. And if, God forbid, we hit a dead end, we'll comb the realms until we bring him home. You have my word."

"I know." Greta's lips thinned into a sad smile. "I just miss him. A lot."

"Me too," I admitted. "I'm here if you want to talk."

"Thanks. And thanks for checking on me. I needed a friend." She took a step backward. "Now, let's get back in the kitchen. I want to be as useful as possible."

With a nod, I followed Greta back to the table. Johann leaned forward on his elbows as we sat.

"So," he summarized, "once we find the ring of volcanoes and identify the one with the cave that opens to the base of the meadow, we locate the second point of entry and move fast."

"That's correct," Hjalmar confirmed. Tore nodded as if he understood, which hopefully meant he'd be able to explain it to me when the time came. "Just know that if Nott's hiding inside Maldraul, she'll have reinforcements stationed in every single exit tunnel. And they'll know to be on the lookout for you."

Well, crap.

"I'd imagine that—" Hjalmar broke off as the device on his wrist started beeping.

"What is it?" Garrett asked nervously.

"Probably just a routine report." Hjalmar glanced at the communicator's screen. "Another heat spell coming from the south; a request for additional coverage at the base; a surge of light energy followed by the opening of a dark portal—*skit.*"

My heart sank. *Skit* was right.

Tore stood so quickly, his chair tipped over behind him. "We have to move," he declared.

"Yup." I jumped to my feet. Mack, Johann, Greta, and Hjalmar did the same.

"But your pie . . ." Garrett frowned.

"The light energy surge is probably one of the pieces of Allie's missing weapon," Tore explained. "Which means the dark portal that opened up most likely brought a search party of dark elves."

"That portal could lead us to Bodie," Greta said fiercely.

Hjalmar glowered. "No night elves enter this realm on my watch."

"Go. All of you." Garrett waved his hands. "Jale and I will clean up."

"Thanks, Dad. Sis." Johann leaned down to kiss his sister's cheek.

"Just be careful out there," she said seriously.

"Always am," Johann said.

We hustled out of the kitchen and strapped into the weapons we'd deposited on the porch. It didn't take long for us to suit up, cut through the village, and follow Hjalmar deep into the forest outside of town.

"The coordinates of the dark burst should be past that rock formation." Hjalmar pointed to a thicket of densely-packed trees. I could just make out a cluster of boulders beyond the shadows.

"Then that's where we're heading." Tore marched determinedly toward the tree cluster, stopping short when Hjalmar pressed a palm to his chest.

"What?" Tore's brow furrowed in confusion.

Hjalmar stared into the shadows. "Do you find it odd that a dark burst erupted shortly after you arrived in Vanaheim?"

Honestly, I just figured we had really, really lousy luck.

"What are you getting at?" Tore asked.

Hjalmar lowered his hand. "Nott's always one step ahead of you, isn't she? You get to a new realm, and she has dark elves in waiting. It's not the first time that's happened, is it?"

A sickening feeling washed over me.

"No. It's not." Johann paled.

Hjalmar released a string of curse words that made the rest of my protectors look like choir boys. "There's a spy in Asgard. I'm sure of it now. Vidar's been looking into it for a while, but whoever's behind this has left no trail."

Tore grimaced at the mention of his father's name. "Do you have any suspects?"

The vein framing Hjalmar's thick neck bulged. "Not yet. But if Revenge doesn't figure this out soon, I will. From now on, trust no one with the details of your missions. Don't send ravens; don't communicate over the wrist coms."

Greta stepped forward. "You think it's someone in the Alfödr's inner circle?"

"They wouldn't." Mack shook his head. "Their oath prohibits—"

"An oath could be manipulated by dark magic." Hjalmar frowned. "I don't know if the traitor comes from the Alfödr's camp, but I do believe Nott could have infected the mind of one of our gods. Or of someone close to one of our gods."

There was a collective intake of breath.

"Nott can infect gods' minds." I shuddered. Until then, I'd been hoping that brand of crazy was limited to dragon and fire-rat possession. *That's where hope got you, Allie.*

"She's a light goddess turned dark, Allie. She can do almost anything." Greta withdrew her crystal wands and held them in front of her in the shape of a cross. If the situation wasn't so dire, I would have laughed.

"Awesome," I whispered.

Tore's arm brushed against mine as he stepped closer. "What do you suggest we do?"

Hjalmar placed his sizeable palm atop the hilt of his sheathed sword. "For now, do nothing. I'll pay Vidar a visit in person, and the two of us will send word when we have more information. Your job right now is to retrieve the pieces of your weapon. If there is indeed a portal in these woods, I, and only I, will be going through it to look for Bodie. Muspelheim is overrun with darkness. The king's guards have been ordered to destroy non-natives on sight, and the dragons have almost doubled in number since my last tour of duty. Either the fire giants are running a breeding program down there, or—"

"Or Nott's infecting them." I groaned.

"I'm not sure if that's possible with animals—"

"It is! Sorry." I cut Hjalmar off with a hastened apology. "But it is possible. When we were on Nidavellir, there was a dragon who'd been . . . I thought she was possessed, but maybe she was infected. Same thing really. Either way, she was definitely a light dragon turned dark. When I killed her, the–"

"You killed a dragon?" Hjalmar's eyebrows shot up.

"Allie has the Liv, Dad. I told you guys a few weeks ago. Try to keep up." Johann sighed.

"Right." A glint came into Hjalmar's eyes, and he looked at me with a little more respect. "You were saying, Allie?"

"Uh, when I killed the dragon, this blackness rose up. Once I destroyed *that*, the light was able to return to her body on its own, and she came back to life."

"You killed and *revived* a dragon?" The corners of Hjalmar's mouth pulled back in a smile. "You are your mother's daughter, aren't you?"

"Eir will be proud of the woman Allie has become," Tore affirmed. At his words, warmth burst from my heart and radiated through my body.

"She will," Hjalmar agreed. "But I meant what I said before. We're about to head into what is most certainly a Nott-laid ambush. And if there is a portal, and if we have reason to believe Bodie is on the other side, then I will be the *only* one crossing through it. Am I clear?"

Hjalmar pierced each of us with his dark-eyed stare. Mack, Johann, and Greta voiced their consent. Tore grunted out a *'ja'* when Hjalmar's eyes met his, and I nodded when the intimidating warrior's gaze bore through me. But I also crossed my fingers behind my back. I didn't like lying to Johann's dad, but he wasn't giving me much of a choice. It was my fault Bodie was gone. If there was a portal that led to him, I was going to go through it.

And I was going to bring him back.

CHAPTER NINE

HJALMAR LED US IN a single-file line toward the concentration of dark energy at the rock formation. Now that we were closer, the energy signature was more discernable. The blackness reached high into the sky, like the ominous tentacles of an octopus. There was definitely a nasty trap waiting for us up ahead. When I relayed my findings to our group, Tore confirmed my assessment.

"Be careful," he warned. "We don't know how many night elves are waiting for us or where they'll be. Stick together."

I moved closer to his side as we continued through the trees. This part of the forest gave way to a small clearing populated by enormous, jagged rocks and a massive tower of boulders. They were stacked on top of one another some fifty feet high, creating a beautiful and bizarre piece of granite art. When we neared the cluster of stone, my armor gave a piercing tingle that radiated from my shoulder to my elbow. Excitement coursed through me as I skidded to a stop.

Tore turned to look at me with concern. "Pepper?"

I rolled my shoulder to lessen the burning sensation. "My armor is going crazy. The piece must be close. Well, that or it's warning me of my impending death."

Hjalmar watched me, an uneasy look in his eye. He raised his head as a gust of wind blew through the trees, bringing with it a smoky scent. His nostrils flared, and he immediately drew two weapons before spinning to face the boulders in a low crouch. "Intruders!" he roared, and my stomach dropped. "Spread out." We all followed his orders without question.

Tore, Greta, and I darted to the left, while Johan and Mack ran to the right. We were too exposed in the clearing, so Tore and Greta dove behind two of the jagged rocks. I was poised to follow suit when a loud crackling drew my attention to the top of the pile.

Holy. Freaking. Hell.

"What in the name of all things evil is that?" My eyes widened as I took in the giant creature. He stood at least fifteen feet tall, with spiky horns atop his head and molten red veins crawling along his body. When the creature bared his yellowed teeth, fire swirled deep within his mouth.

"Some kind of mutated fire giant. Allie, take Greta, and get out of here," Tore commanded.

"But I can help—"

"I want you to protect Greta." Tore cut me off. "She can work her energy magic from the safety of the trees. Head around the rock formation, and hide in the forest. Once I see that Hjalmar's got the monster under control, I'll follow you," Tore promised.

Fine. I grabbed Greta's hand and pulled her forward. "Stay safe," I called over my shoulder before charging past the boulders. Hjalmar and Johann were already halfway to the top, weapons drawn.

"I knew I smelled you," Hjalmar cried. The fierce tenor of his voice echoed through the trees.

A surge of heat nipped at my heels, pushing me to run faster. I released Greta's hand, but she easily kept pace at my side. The flame-flinging beast was a mighty motivator. If that giant was spewing fire, we wanted to get to the forest before the monster singed our escape route.

"What is a fire giant doing in Vanaheim? I thought they were from Moose-heim!" I shouted between labored breaths.

"Muspelheim," Greta shouted back. We pumped our legs harder as we rounded the rock formation and charged for the backside of the boulders. We were nearly to the forest. From there, we'd be able to help our team. God willing.

"Holy hell, do you see that?" I skidded to a stop a few feet away from the tree line. Small bits of gravel lodged beneath my heels as I stared at the swirling black mass on the ground in front of me. A giant portal lay flat on the dirt, spinning with ominous beauty.

Greta sucked in a sharp breath. "If this is the ambush it looks like, then that portal leads straight to Nott. That's where we'll find Bodie."

"Allie!" Tore's cry came from behind me. Before I could respond, a blade pierced the top of my shoulder. *Holy Lord, that hurts!* I dropped to my knees, wincing as I turned to face my attacker. Correction, *attackers*. Five night elves leapt from behind a cluster of rocks and charged at us. *Oh, crap.* This was *so* not good.

I tried to stand, but the burning in my neck sent a searing pain all the way down my spine. Tore emerged from around the rock formation, barreling toward the night elves with his blue sword blazing. But the elves were fast, and I was in a vulnerable position on the ground. Fear crept up my vertebrae, reminding me that I was not only vulnerable like this, but also a liability to my team. *Double crap.* Thankfully, Greta came to my rescue, charging forward with a fierce cry. She slammed her crystal wands together, and an energy burst shot through the advancing night elves, throwing them backwards. Tore swayed on his feet but held his course. By the time I pushed myself up, Tore had cut two of the elves down and was working on a third. Greta unleashed the fury of her wands on the fourth, which left a female with red pits for eyes for me to handle. Since I'd recently cut down and revived a dragon, I knew I could handle one measly night goddess minion.

Even if my body was threatening to self-destruct at any moment. *Step it up, demigod healing. Any time now.*

I drew my sword and took my battle stance. Blood seeped down my arm, but I ignored it, focusing instead on the black energy crawling along the tip of the night elf's sword. I gave an involuntary shiver, never wanting to return to that place again—the place where the darkness held me hostage and threatened to overpower me forever. I desperately hoped my shoulder wasn't infected with that same energy now. I made a note to check it once I'd offed this elf.

"Your soul," the elf seethed, "is mine."

"Then come and get it," I challenged.

The elf leapt forward. Our swords clashed, sending a loud clang ricocheting through the air. "Where's our friend?" I screamed as I swung my blade around. The elf smiled, giving me full view of yellowed, pointy fangs. *Oh, hell no.* Taunting me would be the last thing that demon ever did. I feigned left, and she took the bait, diving for my side and exposing her ribcage. I quickly diverted my blade to pierce her heart. Her eyes widened in shock as blood seeped from her chest, and she fell to the ground, dead.

Relief coursed through me now that my life wasn't in imminent danger. I permitted myself a single shaky inhale before I shut down my feelings and returned to battle-mode. My sword scraped bone as I withdrew it from the elf's carcass, and I flicked my wrist to shake as much blood as possible from the blade. A glance over my shoulder revealed that Tore had eliminated his perp and was moving in to help Greta kill hers. *Good riddance.* When tremors rocked my armor, I spun around and scanned the fifty-foot rock formation. Nestled between the boulders, about halfway up, beamed a light. I couldn't see the monster that surely stood sentinel atop the rocks, but the balls of flame shooting from the top of the boulder-sculpture proved he was there. Johann, Mack, and Hjalmar would have to keep him distracted long enough for me to snatch the piece of Gud Morder, and possibly, join their fire giant assault from behind.

With a steadying breath, I stepped carefully around the portal and scaled the bottom of the sharp rock wall. My shoulder burned like a mother, but I hoped my healing abilities would kick in soon. Grunts and clangs from below suggested that Tore and Greta had a handle on our night elf situation, so I kept my focus on retrieving the weapon piece. Using grooves in the rocks as handholds, I made my way toward the blinding pulse of energy. My boots found purchase on a small ledge that was barely wide enough for the balls of my feet, and I peered between the boulders. *Oh, thank God!* There it was—the titanium tip of my broken weapon flashed from deep between two pieces of rock. Its sharp, pointed end was singular; the boys' sketch must have correctly depicted the twin blades spiraling to make this point. I'd congratulate them when all of this was over. Right after I took a *very* long, fire- and frost-giant-free vacation.

Reaching down, I wedged my hand between the rocks, unceremoniously grabbed the weapon piece, and stuffed it into the satchel at my waist with a silent fist pump.

Four pieces down, four to go.

From my perch halfway up the rocks, I had a clear view of the scene below me. Greta held her wands over the prone body of the night elf while Tore jammed his sword in and out of the monster's throat. Thick blood spurted from an artery, coating Tore's blade in a dense, black goo. Fire sparked in my peripheral vision. My boulder-top protectors must have been taking care of the lone fire giant above me. But it was the black vortex below that drew my attention. From my new vantage point, I was able to see it wasn't the solid black orb it had appeared to be—it was a black, grey, and red swirl, one that held rocky mountains and crackling fire within its depths. It was a window into another land. To Bodie. My heart beat wildly as I stared into the vortex. Our friend was so close—just on the other side of that portal. My armor, my energy centers, *everything* within me knew it to be true.

Johann's victorious cry from above was followed by a deep hiss. The fireballs extinguished, the air filling with a thick layer of ash. A deep boom, followed by a mighty trembling of the earth, signaled the fall of something massive. All signs pointed to the fire giant no longer being a threat. But what would that mean about the portal to his realm? Had he been holding it open, or was something—or someone—doing that from the other side? And more importantly, what did all of this mean for Bodie?

Something warred inside of me, and my eyes sought out Tore's. He stood with one foot atop the freshly-slain night elf, wiping his sword on his cargos and staring intently at me. My throat caught as I glanced back down to the portal. The edges crept inward as it crumbled into itself. Our window to save Bodie was literally closing. With one last glance at Tore, I sent a silent apology, zeroed in on the vortex, and jumped as far from the rocks as I could.

"No, Allie!" Tore blurred into the edge of my vision. He leapt in front of me, so we collided midair. My head whipped to the side, affording me a glimpse of the horror painted across Greta's delicate features. Her hand flew to her mouth, and one leg then the other stretched in front of her as she sprinted after Tore. Was she going to try to follow us? God, I hoped not. The last thing we needed was for Greta to get hurt. *Please, stay put Greta. We need you in one piece.*

Tore's fingers wrapped around my arm, and before I could process anything else the world dropped away from us. We fell, exchanging the atmosphere of Vanaheim for the thick, smoky heat of Muspelheim. A heaviness coated my body as we descended into the dark realm. The ground shot up at us, and Tore pulled me closer to his chest, pivoting so his body was beneath mine. He was going to bear the brunt of our fall, and soon. *Brace yourself, Allie. Here it comes . . .* But just before we struck the ground, the fierce wind whipping my hair calmed, and our bodies dropped to the earth with the force of a mere five-foot fall, not the hundred-foot one we'd just endured. Either Tore had some magical anti-impact abilities he'd forgotten to mention, or we'd gotten a majorly lucky break. As I rolled off of Tore, two crystal wands landed on my stomach. *Greta.* She hadn't made the portal jump, but she'd managed to chuck her energy weapons through to help us out. Bless her. I tucked them into the pouch at my waist, then pushed myself to my feet and faced my wide-eyed protector. He was already up, poised on the balls of his feet, scanning the area for threats.

"I can't believe you just did that," he growled. *Me neither.*

I was about to ask if we were clear when Tore wrapped his fingers around my wrist and pulled me forward. My right big toe caught on the back of my left heel, nearly making me face-plant. But I hopped on one foot until I was able to keep pace with Tore's jog. The dim light of dusk blanketed Muspelheim, but it was light enough for me to scan my surroundings as we broke into a sprint. A large cave was embedded in a massive mountain near our drop site, and a sea of rocky hills towered above us. Their tips spewed fireballs and smoke streams. Had we dropped into a valley of active volcanoes? My heart sank. *So much for that lucky break.*

Without any idea of where we were going, or what we'd do once we got there, I put one foot in front of the other and blindly followed my protector. Tore charged forward, each boot barely touching the ground before lifting off again in a rhythmic run. My gaze darted around the lava-laden land of Muspelheim as I tried not to panic. What had I done? Jumped into a dark portal to hunt down a dark goddess? How insanely stupid had I become? Did I have no sense of self-preservation left? *Bodie. I did it for Bodie.* Surely, we'd be able to save our friend before the volcanoes—or the fire giants—took us out.

Tore rounded the base of a neighboring mountain and called over his shoulder. "We're going up!" Then he dug his fingers into the crevices and began to climb. He tilted his head upward, toward a small opening in the rocks, and I set my focus on the mouth of the cave. I scrambled up the wall behind him, ignoring the fact that my arms and elbows were caked in dust and blood. The only thing I cared about was staying alive long enough to ask Tore how the hell we were going to get Bodie and get out of there without getting killed. Or without incurring first-degree lava burns.

Seriously, Allie, no survival instincts left. None. I'd obviously succumbed to that nervous breakdown I was overdue for.

Once Tore reached the cave, he drew his sword and charged inside. I put my hand on the hilt of my weapon and raced in after him. The space inside was shrouded in darkness, but I didn't need light to see Tore's blue eyes boring into mine with fury. He wanted to kill me.

Did I blame him?

My protector breathed in and out, his nostrils flaring with barely-contained rage. I flashed back to the early days of our relationship, the ones where he hadn't exactly beamed rainbows of love at me. My muscles locked up as I prepared for a verbal throwdown.

When none transpired, I chewed my bottom lip. "I'm sorry?" I offered.

Tore growled an honest-to-goodness growl, and I stepped back.

"Hey, I did this for Bodie! We were looking for a way to find him, and now we have it." I crossed my arms defensively.

Tore's eyes fell to my injured shoulder, and his glare softened. "We were supposed to come here with a battalion of warriors."

Fine. He was right. It was stupid. "Okay, it wasn't my best move. But I saw the portal shutting, and I panicked."

Tore sighed before closing the distance between us. "I know. I was thinking of jumping in, too."

Relief poured through me, and I let go of the breath I was holding. "You were?"

He nodded as he pulled my shirt back to inspect my shoulder. "But then I thought, 'No, that's stupid. Bodie wouldn't want me to go on a suicide mission.' Then you jumped."

"Oh."

Tore's hands cupped my face, and he rested his forehead on mine. "Allie, I love you. But I need you to stop trying to get yourself killed."

My throat tightened as his cool breath washed over my face and his words found their way into my heart. "Never thought the girl who pepper sprayed you in the park would steal your heart, did you?"

Tore's eyes darkened as he eyed my lips. "I did, actually. I knew from the moment I saw you that you would be a giant pain in my butt, and you'd quite possibly be the end of me. In more ways than one."

I stood on tiptoe to give him a soft kiss. "So, what do we do? Call for Heimdall?"

Tore sighed. "I wish. Nott will have spelled Muspelheim so the Bifrost can't drop anywhere near her."

"Does she run this realm, too? I mean, in addition to Svartalfheim?" I asked.

"She doesn't run any realm," Tore corrected. "The Alfödr cast her from Asgard when she turned to darkness, and while she tried to take over Svartalfheim, she was never able to overpower the dark elves. That's why she's so determined to take Midgard from the humans—she wants her own realm to rule."

Not on my watch, Nott.

"We're lucky she's getting impatient," Tore continued. "I'm guessing she's keeping Bodie inside the cave where the portal dropped us. She wouldn't have expected us to kill her fire giant, and she would have wanted a direct route for him to bring you to her. We knew coming in that this was a trap, so we have two options. Option one: we go in solo and try to extract Bodie without being seen. Full risk disclosure: Nott's hideout's probably crawling with night elves and fire giants, and the bad kind of dragons are all over this place. And as you know, we didn't bring any food or water with us. So if we're in there for too long, our bodies will start shutting down. Also, while your shoulder looks okay, we should probably get it checked for a dark magic infection sooner than later."

Awesome.

"What's our other option?" I asked.

Tore paused. "Option two: we still go in after Bodie, but before we do, we try to travel far enough away that we can summon the Bifrost and send for reinforcements. We'll sketch a map at the drop site so our friends will know where to come looking for us. That way, if things go south during our rescue, we'll have backup already *en route*. It will cost us some time. But I think it's prudent to make sure that if we fail Bodie, our friends still have a shot at saving him."

I groaned. "Hiking through Muspelheim with no food or water and hoping we don't die sounds pretty stupid, too." The temperature inside the cave was even more stifling than it was in the volcano-meadow. I was already sweating bullets.

Tore shrugged.

"I wish my pet dragon could just fly us out of here." I laughed, but Tore didn't seem to find my statement amusing. He stared at me intently and eyed the suede pouch at my waist.

"Did you bring the horn?"

I rolled my eyes. "I was kidding. Obviously."

Tore reached out and opened the flap of my pack. Slipping his fingers inside, he withdrew the golden horn. "Remember what Milkir told us? The horn doesn't have boundaries, and neither does Scarlet. If you call her, she'll find a way to get to you. No matter what realm you're on."

"Seriously?" That sounded like something out of a fairytale.

Tore nodded. "So . . . option three. We hike out, summon the Bifrost *and* your dragon, then hustle back and save Bodie's butt. Sound good?"

"It's worth a try," I agreed.

Tore nodded. I could practically see his mind working to pull together all the pieces. We only had one chance to do this right; to rescue Bodie and get out of Muspelheim alive.

With a sigh, I crossed to the mouth of the cave and stared into the red-tinged sky. "Are the constellations the same as the ones we see from Earth? Sorry, Midgard?" Darkness was falling on Muspelheim, but the handful of stars that poked through the red smog bore no resemblance to the Big Dipper or Ursa Major. They shone together in tight clusters, their crimson light different from the white glow I was used to seeing. "If we don't have any kind of navigational marker, how are we supposed to find a safe spot to call the dragon, then get back here without losing track of where Bodie is?" God, I hoped the cave near the drop site was Nott's. If Bodie wasn't in there, we were in even more trouble than I thought.

"*Skit*. Get back." Tore's thick forearm struck my chest as he shoved me behind him.

"Hey!" I protested.

"Quiet," he ordered softly. His footsteps were nearly silent as he herded me away from the opening of the cave and into the darkness of its depths. The steely glint in his eye was enough to tell me that he was simultaneously on alert and excited.

"What's going on?" I whispered.

Tore gave me a look I had zero way of interpreting. But the vein along his jaw bulged as he quietly drew his sword, and I knew something was freaking him out. Bigtime.

"Tore?" I whispered, drawing my own sword.

He met my eyes with a steely gaze, before mouthing the words that sent a fresh wave of terror coursing through every fiber of my over-stressed being.

"It's Nott. She's here."

CHAPTER TEN

MY MOUTH DROPPED OPEN so quickly that my jaw popped. The last thing we needed right then was to be discovered.

Tore tilted his head toward the mouth of the cave. Outside, hurried footsteps scuffed toward our hiding spot. I pressed my back to the rocky wall and tried not to panic at the wave of energetic darkness that washed over me. It was thicker, more cloying, and far more intense than anything I'd sensed from a regulation night elf. My heart pounded, pushing against the fear that threatened to overtake me. I'd already paid my dues to the darkness; no way was I going back to that world of paralyzing despair. I locked down my centers to shield myself from Nott's energy sight. Since Tore was on perpetual lockdown, I knew he'd be invisible to her energetic radar, too.

"What do you mean, you lost her?" The deep, female voice was coarse, as if its owner had endured a lifetime of tobacco use. I was pressed so far against the wall, I didn't have a visual on the voice's owner. But my gut had a pretty good sense.

Nott was close. And she was furious.

"The girl took the bait—she and the demigod came through the portal." The scratchy voice of what I could only assume was a night elf sniveled. "But they vanished without a trace before our ground team was able to retrieve them."

"You were instructed to summon me immediately upon their arrival," Nott bellowed. "Your predecessors more than proved your abilities are insufficient to combat the Asgardians' . . . powers."

"We did summon you." The night elf's voice trembled. "You did not come."

"Liar!" Nott shrieked. "I heard nothing."

I glanced over at Tore. Was the night elf lying? Or was it possible something we'd done had impeded whatever communication the goddess and her minions had in place?

Tore's gaze moved from my face down to my satchel. He pressed a finger to the tan leather, confusion in his gaze. In one swift movement, he raised the fabric of the cover and withdrew one of Greta's crystal wands. Recognition colored his features as he held the tool in his palm. "It's these," he mouthed. Then he quickly waved the wand in front of the pouch, up and down in front of my body, and in a circle around my head. A dense pressure pressed in on my ears as he moved, and the sounds around me became muted—as if I was suddenly underwater.

"What are you doing?" I mouthed the words, not sure what effects whatever Tore had done would have on my voice.

He raised a finger to his lips before repeating the motions along his own body. Then he circled his head with the crystal before tucking the wand back into my pouch. "Cloaking us," he whispered. I furrowed my brow at his distorted tone. He stepped closer so our faces practically touched, and when he spoke again, his whisper sounded normal. "I didn't realize, but it makes sense. Greta must have set the wands to shield before she threw them at us. Our bodies, and now our voices, should be indiscernible to everyone outside of this protection. Not sure how the shield messed with Nott's communication system, but I'll take any advantage we can get."

"So, we're invisible? That's awesome. We don't need my dragon; we can just go get Bodie right now." In my excitement, I flailed my arms and accidentally knocked a rock loose from the cave wall. The sudden growl from outside alerted me to my mistake.

"Where are you going?" the night elf asked.

"Silence," Nott hissed. *Oh, God.* Her footsteps were muted, but they were definitely getting louder.

Tore held the hilt of his sword to his stomach, keeping it vertical with the tip peeking over the top of his head. He stepped in front of me, pressing his back to my chest. His body completely covered my own, so I couldn't see Nott when her voice echoed from inside the cave. But I could feel her. The intensely dark energy that seeped from her being made me want to gag.

"They're close," Nott croaked. My hearing was adjusting to our protection, so Nott's warped words sounded slightly clearer. The hiss of a deep inhale let me know the night goddess was sniffing the air. I desperately hoped Greta's wand-shields covered odor, too. God only knew how awful I smelled after a day fighting fire giants and running from dark elves. *Note to self: invest in demigod-level deodorant before embarking on future missions.*

My plan in place, I peeked my head around Tore's shoulder to catch my first glimpse of the Goddess of Night.

Holy Mother of all things scary. She was terrifyingly close—her bone-thin body stood a few feet outside the base of the cave. Long, black hair tumbled down her rail-thin back, and her arms looked like they desperately needed plumping. But I couldn't deny there was a ghostly beauty in her hollow face. With her black eyes and plump lips, it was easy to see that she had once been stunning. Now, she was nothing more than a shell. She stretched those thin arms over her head and moved her hands in a circular motion. Given what little I knew about her lack of moral compass, I figured she was doing some kind of evil spell. I desperately hoped Greta's crystal-sticks were Nott-proof.

"Do you see them?" The night elf spoke from outside the cave.

"No." Nott continued her hand motions. "But I sense them. They *are* nearby." She turned a slow circle before stepping closer to the inside of the cave, letting her gaze move from the soot-covered floor all the way up to the stone-lined ceiling. I bent quietly to draw my dagger from my boot while Tore kept his sword raised. His muscles tensed against me as Nott pinned us with her black-eyed stare, but the look didn't stick. She completed her visual scan of our hiding spot without lingering any longer than necessary on the two breath-holding demigods huddled together.

Nott turned on one heel with a huff and stormed out of the cave. "Return to the hostage," she seethed. The night elf scurried past the opening to follow her. "No doubt our targets will attempt to retrieve him. We can kill them then."

The footsteps grew quieter until only our shallow breathing filled the cave. When I could no longer sense the energetic blackness of Nott's soul, I permitted myself one shaky inhale. A loud *whoosh* sounded in my ears as I whispered, "Good God. That was terrifying."

"No *skit*. Greta saved our lives." Tore turned to face me, his voice once again at normal volume. He lowered his sword so it dangled at his side. "You okay?"

"Not even a little bit," I answered honestly. "But that doesn't matter. Now we know for sure that Bodie's in this realm. And now we know that Greta's magic wands have super awesome invisibility powers. Thank God you did . . . whatever you did with them. Nott didn't see us."

"They're crystal wands, not magic ones." Tore corrected me with a smile. "And that kind of cloaking device is *very* temporary. The vibrations can only hold for so long. We're lucky they didn't wear off while Nott was in here. Still, we owe Greta a big thanks, don't we?"

"You bet we do," I muttered. I patted my satchel, where the wands now rested safely. They clacked against my dragon horn and the piece of my *other* weapon—the one that would be a lot more useful if *somebody* hadn't broken it into eight pieces. "Guess we'd better call for Scarlet now, huh? If Nott's gearing up for our capture, we don't want to give her any more time to prepare to kill us."

"Agreed." Tore raised his sword so the flat side of the blade rested atop his shoulder. "But we're going to need to trek out a ways to make that call. I don't like being this close to Nott. You remember how loud the horn is. Nott already suspects we're near the mountain somewhere; let's not help her narrow her search parameters."

"Fair enough. I'll follow your lead."

Tore lightly kissed the top of my head and turned for the entrance. I kept my dagger drawn as we walked over Nott's footprints, past a jagged boulder formation. Tore held up a fist, and I came to a silent stop. He peeked around one of the rocks, and with a flick of his wrist we were on the move again. We jogged quietly away from Nott's stronghold and into the rocky forest of Muspelheim. As we traveled, I shot a glance over my shoulder to ensure we weren't being watched. My breath caught at the sight of the huge fire giant patrolling the cave's entrance—no wonder Tore had proceeded with caution. The monster's back was to us, and a further scan revealed no pursuing night elves, but I didn't breathe easier until we were far from Nott's stronghold, hidden deep within the woods. We traveled for at least another hour beneath the smoggy sky, finally stopping at a thick grove of grey-barked trees. Their trunks were charred, and their branches devoid of leaves, as if a fire had ravaged each tree from root to tip. The entire grove reeked of desolation, destruction, and death.

"I hate Muspelheim," I grumbled.

Tore turned around with a smirk. "What ever happened to, 'I love fire. I want to marry fire.' Hmm?"

"When did I ever say—oh, right. Jotunheim." I sighed. "How about we stick to light realm travel once all of this is over?"

"Don't have to ask me twice."

We hiked deeper into the grove. After a short eternity, the foliage gave way to a field of black lava rocks.

"Okay, Pepper." Tore kept his sword drawn. "Call Scarlet. Just pull out your horn and blow."

I bit back a smile. "You know what Bodie would say to that if he was here."

Tore smirked again. "Just do it."

Keeping one hand on my dagger, I withdrew the golden horn from my satchel. I pressed the metal to my lips and exhaled forcefully. A loud baritone rang out, echoing across the lava field.

"God, I hope Nott didn't hear that," I muttered.

"She might have," Tore said casually. "But we're far enough out that it will take her minions a solid couple of hours to figure it out and track us. And by then, we'll be riding Scarlet high above her den."

Seriously, whose hideout was called a den? *Oh, right, a psychopathic night goddess's. That's who.*

"Awesome." I tucked the horn back in my pouch and stared at Tore. "So now what do we do?"

"Now, we strategize. Were you able to catch any of the logistics conversation with Hjalmar?" Tore asked.

"Not much," I admitted. "I was worried about Greta, and I knew you'd fill me in."

"Well, if we're correct about that mountain being Nott's stronghold, then this is what we're looking at." Tore lowered his sword so the tip touched the ashy ground. He used the weapon to sketch a map into the ash at our feet. "Somewhere in that mountain is a den populated by one crazy goddess and a horde of night elves."

"You're not exactly selling the mission so far." I nudged Tore's ankle with my boot.

"No *skit*," Tore agreed. "We need to follow the energy trace into the den. I've never been inside Maldraul Mountain—I'm presuming that's the volcano we dropped in near. But I'm inclined to trust Hjalmar's report of its internal structure."

Tore sketched a series of lines into the soot.

"He said its caverns were numerous but connected to one central location through a series of tunnels. It was once an active volcano, but it's dried up over the years." Tore drew a circle in the center of the lines and marked it with an *X*. "That central location sits underneath an old lava pool that used to run off the nearest volcano. If that's where Nott is keeping Bodie—and since it's a seemingly secure location, it makes sense that it would be—then we can assume Nott's got the entrance to every cavern heavily guarded."

"Then how are we going to get in?" I blew my hair off my forehead in a frustrated puff.

"Hjalmar's secret entrance. The drop zone." Tore's teeth flashed with his grin.

My eyebrows shot to my hairline. I was pretty sure nothing good had ever come from a mission that began at something called 'the drop zone.' "Where are we dropping in from?"

"From here." Tore drew another line with his dagger. "When it was active, the volcano had a second runoff—that channel doesn't connect directly to the central location, but it's separated from it by only a thin layer of sediment. We follow that runoff as close to Nott's lair as we can get, then dig through the wall, jump down into the den, and ambush whatever's waiting on the other side."

"Seriously?" Tore *had* to be kidding me. "You want us to dig through a wall and hope the night elves don't hear us coming?"

"They'll be guarding every other entrance. And the ash walls near the top of the mountain should be pretty easy to kick through." Tore raised one eyebrow. "You got a better idea?"

The pressure in my head built steadily. Everything about this mission was a bad idea. "Fine, Protector. Carry on."

Tore returned his attention to the outline on the ground. "We enter through the mouth of the volcano, then traverse the unguarded trail until we reach the drop zone. It's going to have a horde of guards, but we have enough energy sense between us to feel where they're located. We'll wait for Nott to leave and find a way to disable any night elves that stand in our way."

"Can we hide behind the crystal wand cloak?" I asked.

"We'll try, but we can't count on that." Tore shook his head. "Remember, that shield is based on a vibration, and I don't know how long it will be able to hold inside of a volcano commanded by

Nott. The sulfur dioxide, not to mention the slew of other gasses, may affect the air quality."

"So, we're going in hoping we're invisible but knowing we may have to just . . . fight our way to Bodie?" It wasn't impossible, but I wished we had a better plan.

"Yeah." Tore ran his hands over his head. "That's all I've got at the moment. But we're smart. We'll think of something on the fly."

Right. Because so far, my time in Tore's world had proven me to be an excellent on-the-fly thinker. *Not.*

"Uh, okay." Going in without a concrete plan seemed risky, but I didn't want to leave Bodie on his own any longer than necessary. Worst case scenario, I could use my light whip to do . . . something.

"We'll need to have Scarlet on standby at whichever exit we're able to get to. We won't know which one will be vacant until we go in and see where the night elves flee, so keep your horn on you, and be ready to call her as we're leaving the tunnel with Bodie."

I patted my satchel. "Got it. So, we have an entrance plan, an extraction plan, and a way to get as far away from Nott as possible until we can call the Bifrost to pick us up. What do we do now?"

Tore sat down in the soot and leaned his back against one of the tree trunks. He patted the ground next to him, and I settled into his side. "Now, we wait. It's probably going to take Scarlet a while to get here from Nidavellir. I'm not sure how dragons travel realms, but whatever system they use, it can't be faster than the Bifrost."

"You don't think we should move out now and hope Scarlet will know where to find us? Bodie's been in there for so long already, and—"

Tore silenced me by pressing his lips to mine. I gave myself over to the kiss, but he pulled away much too quickly and continued talking. "We need to ride the dragon to get to the mouth of the volcano. And we need her waiting to fly us out once we rescue Bodie. We don't know what condition he's going to be in, and we can't count on him being able to outrun the night elves. There's no point in rescuing Bodie if he's only going to get recaptured because we didn't set up a proper extraction."

"But is it safe to just wait here like sitting ducks? I mean—"

"I understand your concern. Trust me, Pepper, I don't want Bodie trapped with that monster any longer than necessary, either. And while I appreciate your willingness to go in blind, and frankly, I find it sexy as Hel, we have to be strategic. Going in without an exit plan in place isn't going to do Bodie any favors. And it might cost me the girl I can't imagine existing without.

So, unfortunately, I need us to do things my way on this one."

My breath caught at his words. Yes, I was being bossed around by the world's most irritating demigod. But jeez, did he ever know how to sugar coat a demand.

"Well . . . I guess," I hemmed. Then, because I just couldn't help myself, I blurted, "You're sure this is going to work?"

"I'll take care of you." Tore stroked my hair with one massive hand. "I've been doing this a long time; I'm not going to let anything happen to my girl."

I drew one shaky, acquiescing breath. "Okay."

"Just give me half an hour," Tore said. "If Scarlet doesn't show by then, we move out and figure out a new plan. Close your eyes; see if you can get some rest."

Ha! Rest at a time like this. "Yeah, right."

"Your demi system will rejuvenate in that time, and your shoulder should be fully healed when you wake up—though I still want Greta to look at it. Hopefully Scarlet will be here by then, and we'll go save our friend. Rest's an order, Pepper."

"You don't get to order me around," I chided him. Tore may have held court back at Protector Palace, but if he thought he got to be the boss of me—beyond the Bodie extraction deal—he had another thing coming.

"Then I'm asking you." He lowered his head so his eyes were level with mine. Clear-blue orbs bored into my soul with an intensity I wasn't prepared for. "Please do what you have to do to be at your best for what I hope is the deadliest situation I'm ever going to ask you to walk into. I don't want you getting hurt."

Well, when he put it like that . . .

"Fine," I agreed. "I'll close my eyes. But I can't guarantee I'll sleep. There's kind of a lot on my mind, you know?"

"I know." Tore grimaced. "But any rest you can get will be good for you. Trust me."

I nestled my head against his shoulder, closing my eyes as I threw my arm around his waist. I trusted Tore just fine.

It was the horde of monsters waiting somewhere inside that volcano that I didn't trust.

CHAPTER ELEVEN

I DIDN'T EXACTLY SLEEP, though exhaustion did pull my body into a weird half-awake state. But the moment Tore shifted his shoulder, my eyelids sprang open, and I gave a soft gasp. There, in the air right before us, hovered a shimmering blue energy. I scrambled to my feet, careful not to slip on the sharp lava rocks. Tore slowly pushed himself up beside me, and we both watched in utter fascination as the blue energy took on a larger, more defined form. In moments, Scarlet had materialized right before us. Dragon magic was seriously awesome.

When Scarlet's talons hit the ground, she made a chuffing noise and looked around frantically. She exhaled forcibly when she saw me, so I quickly stepped forward to stroke her sleek scales.

"Good girl," I murmured as I patted Scarlet's neck. She all but purred in reply.

A glance over my shoulder confirmed Tore was watching me. His expression was indecipherable. "What?" I asked.

Tore blew a stream of air through his lips. "To be honest, I wasn't a hundred percent sure that was going to work out."

Great. We were all about winging it right now.

"What do we do? Scarlet's here, so we can go straight to Bodie, right?" Nott was probably scouting for us, and Bodie was probably being tortured. The faster we could all get out of here, the better.

"Almost." Tore removed the dagger he kept tucked into his boot. "First, you need to bond with the dragon."

I raised one eyebrow. I *so* did not like the way Tore was cleaning his blade on his pants. "Like, have a special chat and become besties? That kind of bonding?"

He shook his head. "You haven't completed your bond. I imagine Milkir was going to walk you through it back on Nidavellir, but we didn't get the chance. And since we need to be able to ride your dragon, you need to bond with her. Now."

I swallowed hard. "And that dagger is somehow involved in this bonding?"

Tore shrugged. "That's what Mack told me years ago. It's worth a try."

I groaned. "Today is the day of experiments."

Tore asked for my hand, and I held it out. At this point, I had had so many injuries it wasn't the pain I was worried about. It was the *bonding*, whatever that entailed.

As if she could sense my anxiety, Scarlet nuzzled her face into my tummy. She was a good egg. Without explaining anything, Tore sliced the knife across the top of my forearm. When I yelped, my dragon flared her nostrils and shot Tore a murderous look.

"It's okay," I told her.

Tore looked wearily at Scarlet before handing me the dagger. "Now slice her. Quickly before you heal."

Oh, God. I knew that was where this was headed. "Sorry, girl," I muttered. I knelt to put my hands on her front foot. I was careful not to cut too deeply, and she barely flinched when the blade sliced through a few of her red scales. When a few pearlescent drops ebbed from the wound, I looked up at Tore. "Now what?"

"Quick, rub the cuts together." Tore gave my back a gentle nudge.

"This is weird," I said. Scarlet blinked down at me with puppy-dog eyes, probably wondering why I'd had to cut her. I was wondering the same thing myself.

Here goes nothing.

I pressed my open cut to hers and held my breath. The second our blood commingled, I was thrown backward with a searing headache.

"Ahh!" I grabbed my head, breathing in through my teeth while pain ricocheted across my brain like a pinball.

"*Skit*! Allie, I'm sorry." Tore came to my side. But just as quickly as the headache had come, it was gone and . . .

'Master,' a bold female voice spoke into my mind. I yelped, scrambling backward, away from Tore and Scarlet. My mouth dropped open as my pet dragon, head held low, stared into my eyes.

'Scarlet?' I tried.

Did she smile? *'Yes, Master.'*

My eyes nearly popped out of my head as I jabbed an accusatory finger at Tore. "You!"

He blanched. "What happened?"

I leapt to my feet, keeping my finger pointed at Tore. "She is speaking *into my mind*. You are paying for all of my therapy for forever, do you understand me?"

The tension drained from Tore's face. "Good, you are bonded. We need a ride. Ask her to fly us far enough away from Maldraul Mountain that we can call the Bifrost."

I took a steadying breath. I could yell at Tore later. After I had saved Bodie with my mind-reading pet dragon. *Therapy for life.*

'Uh, Scarlet? We need to ride you. Is that okay?' I pressed the thoughts into my dragon's mind, while my sense of self-preservation all but screamed, *Please say no. I'm so scared.*

Unfortunately for my survival instinct, my dragon bowed down low. *'Yes, Master. We fly.'*

I frowned. *'Call me Allie.'*

'Yes, Master Allie. We fly now.'

With a sigh, I passed along the message. "She says we can fly her."

Tore grinned. "Nice."

I took a few tentative steps towards the big beast. She knelt awkwardly before us, her barbed tail raised in the air. My gaze skimmed her back until I found the place where her wings met between her shoulder blades. Reaching up, I ran my hand along the grooves there.

Scarlet purred. Like, a legit purr. Telling myself anything that purred couldn't be dangerous, I studied Scarlet's back for possible riding spots. The safest place to sit seemed to be just behind Scarlet's wings but in front of the spikes that began at the base of her tail.

'Hurry, Master Allie. I smell darkness. Must keep safe.'

My eyes bugged, and I scrambled awkwardly onto the dragon's back, wincing as one of her spikes jammed painfully into my thigh.

"Hurry up. She smells darkness. Nott must be coming," I relayed.

Tore took one step towards Scarlet and my dragon hissed, sending a puff of smoke through her nose.

"Hey, be nice. That's my boyfriend," I scolded.

'He cut you.'

Oh, for heaven's sake. *'He cut me to bond us. He protects me. Like you do. Be nice.'*

Scarlet lowered her body with a frustrated chuff, allowing Tore to jump on behind me.

Tore wrapped his arms around my waist. "This feels weird. I should be in the front."

Laughter bubbled in my throat. "My dragon. I drive." While Tore grumbled behind me, I turned my attention to Scarlet. *'Let's fly. Take us away from the source of the darkness. I'll tell you when to land.'*

At my thought, the dragon's bat-like wings kicked out, their flapping making my hair fly in all directions. Without another word, Scarlet's body rose from the ground, and we were airborne.

Holy mother. I was flying my pet dragon across Muspelheim. Every time I thought my life couldn't get any weirder, we went and upped the crazy.

As we flew farther from Maldraul Mountain, the desolate realm passed beneath us. Muspelheim was barren, no doubt. But there was a beauty in the way the lava oozed off the tops of its mountains and the way the rocks jutted out of the stark earth. The whole effect was mesmerizing, in a post-apocalyptic kind of way.

"Tore!" I shouted through the wind. "How long do we have to fly to be in Bifrost range?"

He was silent for a moment. "Maybe another fifteen minutes if the dragon flies fast."

I directed Scarlet to fly fifteen minutes south, continuing her trajectory away from Maldraul Mountain. When we reached our destination, I asked Scarlet to ground us near a pool of dried up, blackened lava. She landed us safely inside a nearby cavern. The overhanging rocks shielded us from any fire giants, or night elves, or God knew what else may have been roaming around.

Tore shifted behind me, sliding as if he intended to get off of Scarlet. I reached back to stop him.

"Wait." I unstrapped my brown suede waist pouch and handed it to Tore, keeping only Scarlet's horn in my hands and Greta's crystal wands tucked into the waist of my pants. "Just call the Bifrost and have Heimdall send this back to the safe house."

Tore's brows knitted together. "You're afraid Nott will steal the piece of Gud Morder?"

I nodded. "I'm also hoping that if our S.O.S somehow gets misdirected or lost in translation, the team will see this pouch whenever they get back to Canada and know to ask Heimdall to direct them to our last known Bifrost drop."

Tore leaned forward to kiss me. "Always have a failsafe. Genius." He slid off my dragon and stepped a few feet away before pulling out his dagger. He bent low and carved some lines into the ashen, black surface. It wasn't until he labeled the Bifrost site and Maldraul Mountain that I figured out he was drawing a map leading to Nott's hideout, just like we'd talked about. When our friends dropped in, they'd know just where to find us.

I hoped.

With the map in place, Tore stepped outside the cavern and summoned the Bifrost. Meanwhile, I sent silent prayers to any deity who might be open to requests, begging them to let our crazy plan work. After an agonizing ten seconds, the Bifrost shot down in front of the cavern, illuminating the space in a spectacle of light. Tore chucked the pouch containing the piece of Gud Morder into the rainbow and shouted out instructions to Heimdall. When the pouch was gone and the rainbow withdrew from sight, Tore jumped onto Scarlet's back.

"Let's get the Hel out of here," he ordered.

I relayed new flying instructions to my dragon, and we were once again airborne, *en route* to Maldraul Mountain.

As we soared across Muspelheim, and in all likelihood toward our imminent death, I took some comfort in knowing that if we perished trying to save Bodie, Mack and the boys would come in and fix our mess.

****

A quarter of an hour later, Tore, Scarlet, and I hovered atop the mouth of the allegedly dormant volcano that was Maldraul Mountain. Scarlet's wings flapped fiercely against the wind that kicked hot flames in oversized swirls away from the lava.

"What is that? You said this volcano was dried up!" I screeched into Tore's ear.

He gave my shoulders a gentle squeeze. "Nott must have reactivated it. Doesn't change the plan."

The plan had been for Scarlet to drop us atop a *dried up* volcano. Now, I instructed her to get us as close to the edge as she could without singing her leathery hide. We'd have to figure out how to drop onto the narrow ledge without teetering into the molten fire.

Didn't change the plan, my left foot. *Men.*

As Scarlet neared the mountain edge, Tore launched himself from our ride, landing gracefully on the narrow mountaintop. He held out his arms and called up to me. "Remember, Allie—jump left, the wind will—"

"I know, it's going to blow right. Got it." I swung my leg over Scarlet's back and focused on my target.

'Thanks for the ride girl,' I patted the scales along her neck.

Since there was no way to slow my pounding heart, I prayed the palpitations would improve my focus. Then I pushed off my dragon, aiming to land just to the left of Tore. As predicted, the wind blew me away from my intended target, so I dropped neatly into the awaiting arms of my protector. He caught me with ease and lowered me onto the ledge beside him.

"Now what?" I asked.

"Now we take a little hike." Tore glanced at the sky. "Tell Scarlet to wait for us nearby. We'll call her when we're ready to move with Bodie."

'Scarlet?' I spoke to my telepathic reptile friend. This relationship was beyond weird.

'Yes, Master Allie?' my dragon sent back.

'Just Allie's fine. Seriously.'

'Yes, Master Just Allie?' came Scarlet's reply.

'No, I mean . . . oh, forget it. Master Allie wants you to wait up here. I will call for you when we have our friend. But I won't know where at the base of the mountain I'm going to be, so can you just follow the sound of the horn for me?'

'We bond, Master Allie. I know your location. Always.'

Oh. Right. Dragon master perk.

Scarlet flapped her wings and moved far enough from the flames that she was no longer in danger of becoming reptilian flambé. She landed on a narrow outcropping of rocks that shouldn't have been able to support her massive frame, yet somehow did. Maybe the whole dragon magic deal was more powerful than I thought

"All right, Scarlet's on standby. I'll follow you in." I gave Tore a tight nod.

"Wait." He bent down to swipe three fingers in a pool of jet black ash. "Close your eyes."

"We're on narrow ground; I don't really think that's the smartest—oh." I squeezed my eyes shut as Tore pressed his fingertips above my left eyebrow and drew them down along my cheek. *Weird.* I didn't open my eyes until he'd removed his hand. "Is this some demigod good luck ritual?"

"Kind of." Tore dipped one finger back into the ash. He traced a line downward from my bottom lip, before cradling my chin between his thumb and forefinger. "Asgardian warriors wear paint when they go into battle." He stepped back to study me. "Just like I thought. Sexy as Hel. Now let's move."

Oh my God, could he be any hotter?

Without another word, he jumped from the ledge onto a narrow track that rimmed the volcano in a two-story spiral. We walked carefully forward, hugging the toasty rocks of the mountain wall to avoid falling into the lava down below. Heat pulsed up in waves, lining my brow with sweat. Nott must have been beyond powerful, if she could re-activate a dormant volcano. God only knew the kind of havoc she could wreak on Earth. We seriously needed to bring her down.

At the end of the path, we stepped cautiously into the blackened opening of a tunnel. "Is this our entrance?"

"Yep." Tore drew his sword, and its blue luminescence lit the tiny space. The tunnel was narrow—barely wide enough for us to fit through and so shallow that Tore would have to duck as he walked. "This is the dead-end Hjalmar told us about. We should be able to sense the dark energy coming off Nott's den when we're near it. And I'll be able to sense Bodie. I've been able to identify his signature since we were kids."

"So, go in blind, sense energy through walls, find Bodie, grab him and go. Easy peasy." I drew my own sword, appreciating the illumination brought to it by Valhalla's finest. "Okay, let's go."

Tore bent down to plant a light kiss on my lips. "Be careful, Pepper. And don't forget, you're Eir's daughter."

I used the hand that wasn't holding my sword to reach up and grab the back of Tore's head. I pulled his mouth to mine and kissed him thoroughly. After a delicious half-minute of contact, I pulled away. "I love you," I said breathlessly.

"I love you, too," he murmured. We were *not* saying goodbye. Because we were *not* going to die in this mountain. We just weren't.

Tore stepped into the tight space with a sigh. "We're really going to need that vacation after this, aren't we?"

"The clothing optional one?" I allowed my anxiety to be replaced with a searing pulse of desire. *Mmm. Clothing optional.*

"*Ja,* that one." Tore moved forward.

I crept after him. "The minute we kill Nott, let's book that puppy."

"Already on it." Tore continued walking, so I followed him into the darkness. The further we moved into the tunnel, the hotter it got. Apparently, this track ran adjacent to another runoff. Since the volcano was supposed to have been dormant, this would have been the perfect hidden entrance to Nott's hideout. But with fiery liquid running somewhere on the other side of the stone, the temperature was stifling. And it would only get hotter as we went deeper into the mountain. I crept closer to Tore, who was still talking about our maybe-if-we-don't-die vacation.

"I have a private villa in Bora Bora reserved for three different weeks over the next six months," he continued. "We're bound to make one of the reservations."

The toe of my boot struck a hard object, and I nearly face-planted into Tore's back. I lowered my sword so it lit up the rocky floor and kept a closer watch on my feet. "You really think this'll all be over within six months?"

"If I have my way, it'll be over within six days. My first reservation is a week from today." Tore reached back to touch my arm. "Careful, I see an overhang that dips up ahead. We might have to crawl."

"Great." *Because hunching through an uncomfortably hot, sulfur-scented volcano tunnel isn't fun enough. Let's add scraping our hands and knees on some rocks to the mix.*

"You got this, Allie. I promise," Tore assured.

I dropped onto my knees, shifting my sword so I could crawl on my elbows. The spectacular view I now had of Tore's butt very nearly made up for the sharp pains I endured with each piercing rock that stabbed through my pants.

Almost.

"We should be getting close. Either the tunnel takes a sharp turn up ahead, or I'm seeing the dead-end Hjalmar told me about." Tore crawled forward a few more feet, then paused. "Do you sense anything?"

I reached out with my energy, pushing it through both sides of the rock wall. On my right, I sensed nothing but heat—it must have been that stupid, re-activated lava stream that ran parallel to our path. But sure enough, on the left, a cloying black energy nudged against mine. "Yes," I confirmed. "I sense three . . . no, four presences. But they've got pretty normal amounts of darkness in them—I don't sense that awful energy of Nott's, just her minions."

Tore swung his legs around so he sat on his butt. He placed one hand to the left side of the wall and closed his eyes. When he opened them, the blue light of his sword reflected in his pupils. "I feel her. You're right; she's not in the open space on the other side of the wall. She's in one of the tunnels, I think. Her signature is moving away from us."

"Then we'd better go now, while we still have the chance. Can you sense Bodie?" I pushed my signature out again but couldn't pick up any trace of the blue-green energy that was our friend.

Tore furrowed his brow. "I'm not sure. There's a flicker on the far wall of the den that feels almost like him, but it's laced with so much darkness . . . *skit.*"

"What?" It was never good when Tore swore.

"His energy's been compromised. Remember how the darkness overtook you on Jotunheim? When your memories were wiped, and you didn't know where you were?"

I shuddered. "How could I forget?"

"I think that's what's happening to Bodie. There's a very slight trace of his energy, but it's littered with so much darkness I can barely recognize his essence. That means it will have been all but lost to him. We need to get him out *now* and get him to Greta. Gods willing, the two of you can extract the darkness." Tore pushed himself onto his knees. He grasped his sword and placed the tip against the wall. "I'm going to break through. Once there's a big enough opening for us to squeeze through, I'll drop in and take care of the night elves. Your sole job is to get to Bodie and blast him with whatever tools you have. Shoot him up with the Liv, or use your whip to kill off the darkness, whatever your gut says will work. He doesn't have much time left."

Crap. No wonder I hadn't been able to sense him. "What if Nott comes back?"

"I'll take care of her. I'll take care of *everyone*," Tore vowed. "You just take care of you and Bodie. Promise me."

I met his too-intense gaze. "I promise."

I took a deep breath and called the Liv into my chest. Since we had very little idea of what we were walking into, I wanted the Liv on call when we dropped in on that den. *Please, don't let me die before Bora Bora.* "Okay. Go on three."

Tore met my look, determination in his eyes. "Just focus on Bodie," he reminded me. "I'll have your back."

"You always do," I said. And I knew it was true. Whatever happened, I knew that Tore would always protect me. It wasn't just his job anymore—it was his purpose.

And preserving the light in our realms—and in our friends—was mine.

"One." I nodded.

"Two," Tore continued. "Three."

Oh, God. Here we go again.

CHAPTER TWELVE

WITH ONE FIERCE MOVEMENT, Tore drove his sword through the wall. He whipped it through the rock in a *Z* shape, then stuffed the blade back into his sheath. Raising his fists, he pounded through the rocky barrier with fierce jabs and launched himself through the rubble and into Nott's hideout. I dove after him, dropping about three feet down before landing on the balls of my feet. I whipped my head from side to side as I scanned the area for our friend. Before I located Bodie, a dark shape launched itself into my peripheral vision. Tore cut my attacker down before he could lay a hand on me.

"Go, Allie!" he shouted.

I needed no further encouragement. In seconds, I was back on my feet and running. We'd landed in a cavernous room, off of which three hallways led into the larger network of tunnels. Sconces lit up the walls with containers of suspended lava—no doubt Nott had enchanted the glass so it wouldn't melt under the intense heat. Slowing to a walk, I closed my eyes and opened my second sight until a dying pulse of blue-green energy registered on my left. *Oh, Bodie. What has she done to you?*

I moved through the cavern with my sword raised in front of me and entered the hallway on the left. Opening my palm, I called forth the Liv and quickly molded it into shape. My whip crackled to life in my hand, and I held it high as I continued forward. My footsteps slowed as I neared a bend in the tunnel, and I knew I was close to my friend. An ever-dimming blue-green light was being choked out by the blackest energy I had ever sensed. Oh, God. What if I wasn't strong enough to fix this? *You're the daughter of Eir,* I reminded myself. *Tore believes in you. Now you have to believe in yourself.* Without another moment of hesitation, I burst around the corner.

And I realized the dimming blue-green light was a trap.

"Allie, run!" Bodie shouted. He was tied to a chair that was chained to the wall. He was cut up, bloody, and covered in black soot—he looked like he'd been to hell and back. But he was very much alive and not at all possessed by the darkness. *Thank God.*

"Bodie, you're okay!" I raced to his side, but he swung out a leg and swept my feet out from under me. My light whip flickered and died. "Ouch! Why would you—"

"Stay down!" he yelled. I flattened my stomach to the gravel just as a black streak of dark energy whipped past my head.

Oh. That's why.

"Thanks," I called as I rolled onto my side. The tunnel looked clear, so I popped up and positioned myself directly in front of Bodie's chair. I regenerated the Liv just as Nott strolled around the corner, a freaky, black energy whip in her hand. It sizzled with a darkness so heavy, it smothered everything in the room. Nott's weapon would have been designed to destroy light, to choke the goodness out of whatever it touched. It would destroy Bodie and me, if I let it. But I wasn't going to do that—not when I had its energetic opposite.

With a flick of my wrist, I brought my light whip to life and stared into the hollow eyes of the Goddess of Night.

Bring it on, Nott.

"Allie, Allie, Allie." Nott's voice had the grating tones of gravel scraping a chalkboard. "What am I going to do with you?"

I *was not* having a conversation with this psycho. I cracked my whip at her, but she quickly cast her weapon in my direction to counter my move. The two whips collided midair, tangling into a thick, glowing knot. *Crap.*

The dark goddess grinned. "The Liv is such a fascinating thing. As you surely know, darkness is the absence of light. And the more light I destroy, the more powerful my darkness becomes. Your mother learned that lesson the hard way."

Rage boiled within me at the mention of my mom. I yanked my whip hard, forcing Nott to stumble forward. As she adjusted her grip on her weapon, I wondered how I was going to get Bodie out of here without getting us both killed. I ran through possible attack plans in my mind while I scanned Nott's energy for any kind of weakness. The swirling darkness consumed every inch of her being like a head-to-toe onesie made up of agitated bees. She was lost to the darkness, and it was far too powerful to allow any weakness in.

Attacking Nott was out. Bodie and I would just have to make a run for it.

I wrenched my whip again, and a pulse of blue Liv shot through the knot that connected my weapon to Nott's. The darkness surged, creeping toward the Liv, and constricting so its brilliant blue light faded to a powdery shade.

Think. Think. Think. What would Greta do?

It came to me in a flash, and I used my free hand to reach behind my back. "You know I'm kind of disappointed. I thought you'd be *way* more powerful."

Nott's nostrils flared, and her eyes blackened so they matched the soot-covered ground. While she seethed, I wrapped my fingers around the two crystal wands that were stashed inside my waistband. And I waited.

"You're a fool!" The walls shook with Nott's cry. "You have no idea what I'm capable of."

I wasn't sticking around to find out. I charged the crystals with the Liv and flung them from behind my back in one quick move. One of the crystals went wide, but the other cracked Nott right in the forehead. Her whip fizzled and died, freeing mine from its deadly grasp. With new-found freedom, I pulled my arm back and cracked my whip at Nott's arm. Her shrill scream filled the small space, sending a chill down my spine. I didn't let up; if I did, Bodie and I would both be dead. Gud Morder was the only weapon that could destroy Nott. But beating her down with the Liv would buy us enough time to escape with our lives.

Or so I hoped.

Each lash of my whip left huge, red welts across Nott's body. The blackness of her energy lightened with each strike, and pieces of the darkness leapt off her body as if recoiling from the Liv. I had no idea how I was going to maintain my assault *and* manage to untie Bodie, but I couldn't let up on Nott. Footsteps sounded behind me, and my freak-out morphed into a full-fledged panic. If a night elf burst in here now, we were so royally screwed. Why had I gone and poked the Goddess of Crazy?

When the large, bearded figure burst into the tunnel, I nearly cried. Mack looked back and forth from me to Bodie. What he saw couldn't have given him much hope—me cutting into Nott like she was a Thanksgiving turkey and Bodie bloody and broken, tied to a chair that was strapped to a wall. He must have surmised my protector needed his help more than I did, because he crossed to the chair and untied Bodie.

My concentration faltered as Bodie crumbled to the ground, and Nott took the opportunity to force her power on me. Though she was twenty feet away, and though I'd thought I'd done a decent job of shielding myself, Nott raised one hand and yanked my body into the air. My whip disappeared as Nott jerked me from side to side, then slammed me into a wall. *Good God, that hurts!* She rose from her spot on the ground, gliding toward me with a snarl as I lay slumped against the crumbling ash wall. *Holy nightmare of all nightmares.* Pain shot up my back, but I forced myself to stand, reinforcing my energetic shield as I moved. Nott was just a few feet from me now, and Mack was struggling to help Bodie up. I cracked my whip to life again, but I was too slow to prevent Nott from launching a dark blob at me. I ducked out of the way, but it grazed the top of my shield. Oh, God, what did that mean?

"Fear," Nott whispered to the darkness. The tentacles of the black blob hooked into my shield as anxiety crept over me, choking out my confidence. Sticky sweat covered my palms, and unfamiliar thoughts barged across my brain. Tore would cheat on me with his sexy ex, Synna. The boys were only my friends because they took an oath to protect me. Everyone would leave me, and I would live my life alone. No parents. No children. No family. *Alone.*

The fear consumed me, and the Liv ebbed from my chest. Nott flared her dark whip to life and advanced toward me, but I did nothing to stop her. I couldn't—I was paralyzed, held in place by a mind-numbing terror.

Everyone I loved would be taken from me. Just like they had always been.

As I blinked against the tears, a blond blur with a massive sword jumped in front of me.

"Nott!" Tore shouted, bringing his sword down hard on the black whip. It flickered, then disappeared, retreating from the blazing blue light of Tore's blade. "Hold on, Allie," he called to me. "We're going to get you out of here."

His words gave me the strength to push back against the blackness. I called the Liv back into my chest and sent it through my palm to push against the black tentacles. They hissed against my shield before detaching and dropping onto the floor. The moment they left, the fear released its hold, and I was once again filled with light, and purpose, and love.

We were getting Bodie the hell out of here. Also, Nott had to die.

Suddenly, a hand on my arm pulled me backward. I wrenched myself free to whirl on my attacker.

"It's just me, Allie. We have to go," Mack urged. He supported Bodie in one arm and held the other out to me.

"No way. I'm not leaving Tore." I stepped backward. "Get Bodie out of here. We'll follow as soon as we can."

With a nod, Mack slung Bodie's arm around his shoulders. Then he raced down the tunnel, dragging our limping friend to safety. When they were out of sight, I cracked my whip to life and crossed to Tore's side. He had backed Nott against the wall, and his blue sword was poised to strike. I knew the weapon wouldn't kill her, but I *seriously* hoped it could disable her long enough for Tore and me to book it out of that tunnel without being followed. I'd just raised my arm, intending to lash Nott until the will to chase us left her, when a fierce voice rang out from behind me.

"Nott, fallen goddess of Asgard! In the name of Odin the Alfödr, you are under arrest!"

My head turned in the direction Mack and Bodie had gone, and I gasped at the sight of a half dozen warriors. Four men and two women pulled glowing blue blades from sheaths at their backs. They glowered at the night goddess with war-painted faces that all but screamed *I will cut you.* Since their swords matched Tore's and they seemed to be on our side, I could only assume Revenge's backup had arrived. And they were all kinds of scary.

"Stand down, Nott," the tall female commanded. She stepped forward, her sword pointed at Nott's chest. Her unit advanced with her, and a flicker of fear flashed in Nott's eyes before it gave way to malice.

The monster cackled as she tilted her head back. The sound grated on my last nerve. Her thin, red-slashed body shrunk, and black feathers popped up on her arms. *What?* It took only seconds for Nott to transform herself into a flock of demonic-looking birds, each with a pair of beady red eyes. They scattered, sending all of us diving for the ground. I didn't want to touch them—who knew what kind of evil energy they carried? Icy terror sloshed in my gut as the birds flew quickly through the tunnel and disappeared.

"Birds? What the hell?" I exclaimed.

Tore rushed to my side. He was covered in blood and soot but otherwise looked to be okay. "Are you all right?"

"Yup," I lied. I was *so* not okay. I'd just looked into the face of evil, lived through my worst fears, and seen things I could never unsee. Plus, birds.

'Scared. Master Allie okay?' Scarlet's voice invaded my head.

I whirled around to address the Asgardian warriors. "My pet dragon's freaking out. Let's get outside."

The crew looked at me like I was crazy, but in all honesty, I was freaking out, too. I needed to get out of there, make sure Bodie was okay, and decompress from fighting Nott. I hurriedly grabbed my crystal wands from the ground and slid them into the waist of my pants. Tore slipped his hand into mine and led me through a maze of tunnels. Every so often, we passed the crumpled carcass of a dead night elf. *Ew.*

"How did a half-dozen people take down Nott's stronghold?" I whispered to Tore as the warriors followed behind us. I must have counted twenty dead elves already.

Tore shook his head. "This was just a trap. Like I told you before, Nott's stronghold is on Svartalfhiem. We would never be able to infiltrate that this easily."

Right. We still had that little pleasure cruise to look forward to.

Light shone up ahead as we snaked our way toward the exit. The moment I crossed the threshold of the tunnel, I sucked in deep lungfuls of sulfur-laden air and let the warm breeze wash over me. *I'm okay. It's over . . . for now.*

My gaze fell on my rescued protector, and I leapt forward, tackling him in a tight hug. "Bodie!"

"Ow!" His laugh-cry was muffled by my shoulder.

"Oops, sorry." I pulled back just enough to scan his energy. It looked okay, no dark blobs. But his wrists were bloody and bruised, and his normally jovial demeanor had given way to a haunted look.

"Oh, Bodie." I gently squeezed his arm. "What did she do to you?"

Tore nudged me aside to give Bodie a careful hug. "*Hei*, man. Glad you're back."

"You and me both." Bodie shuddered. "I'm okay, Allie. Greta fixed me up."

I looked past him to find the red-haired healer petting Scarlet. She looked like she was wrestling with something. I had to imagine it was hard for her to see Bodie like this. It was hard for any of us.

'Like her.' Scarlet told me.

'I like her, too,' I agreed.

I slipped my hand into Bodie's and squeezed lightly. His lost expression faded the tiniest bit. I flared the Liv to life and let it pulse from my hand into his. He looked down at his feet, his cheeks reddening in . . . was that embarrassment?

"It's okay," I told him. "None of this was your fault."

Bodie nodded, breathing deeply as the blue light traveled up his arm and settled into his heart.

"The physical torture was manageable. But she messed with my head, too," he admitted. His voice cracked over the words.

Johann and Mack flanked Bodie. They each placed a hand on one of his shoulders.

"You're safe now," Tore told him.

Bodie nodded, but I knew it would be a while before he believed it was true. Some injuries were invisible; I understood that better than most. I'd grown up without parents, and when Gran died, I'd fought hard to keep from drowning in loneliness. Nott had tapped into and preyed upon that pain. Whatever fears Nott had triggered in Bodie had been active before she'd gotten to him.

If he was like most of us, he'd live with them for a long time—but I had faith he'd be able to manage them again, now that he was outside Nott's influence. As I sent pulses of the Liv through his heart, he looked much more like his normal self. *Good.*

"There you go. You've got some color on your cheeks now." I squeezed his hand before letting go.

Bodie turned to me with one of his devilish looks and winked. "That's what she said."

I just laughed. Our Bodie was back. Nott may have bent him, but she hadn't broken him. Thank God.

Tore turned to face the wave of guards that had assembled at the mouth of the tunnel. The original six had been joined by four more, and now that I had time to check them out . . . good Lord, they were hot. There were seven guys and three girls. The guys were undeniably handsome—like firefighters on a calendar handsome. They were all bulging muscles and chiseled jaws. The girls, well they were gorgeous and intimidating, especially the tall, red-haired one with the jagged scar over one eyebrow. My eyes lingered on the network of braided scars that trailed down her arm. I wondered what had happened to her.

"Let's get you home." Tore clapped Bodie on the back.

"Incoming!" the tallest of Revenge's warriors shouted.

I spun around to see one of Nott's black birds beelining it right for me. My breath caught in my throat as I pulled my blade and brandished it, ready to take the bird's head clean off.

"Relax, Allie. It's Huginn." Tore's hand snaked out and forced my blade down.

My bad.

With a nervous laugh, I sheathed my weapon as Huginn dropped a scroll at my feet. Tore bent down to retrieve it as Scarlet huffed at the raven.

'*He's a friendly,*' I scolded her. Not that I really had any place to scold her since I'd nearly beheaded the Alfödr's raven. But if we were ever going to bring her to live with us, we'd need to work on my dragon's manners.

Tore finished reading the scroll and clenched his jaw. "I need a volunteer to take Bodie home and see that he fully recovers. The rest of us need to head to the black pits to retrieve the piece of Gud Morder that, apparently, is being guarded by fire giants."

My mouth popped open. *Seriously?* I needed a freaking break. And some food, and a shower, and Bora Bora.

"I'm fine." Bodie tried to resist, but Tore just shook his head.

"I volunteer to go with Bodie." Greta stepped forward. She wrung her hands nervously.

"Okay, I'll go back." Bodie answered so quickly, I couldn't help but feel a little lighter in my heart. We may have been about to go into another potentially life-ending situation, but if Bodie and Greta could finally confront their feelings for each other, then I could die happy.

Johann and Mack tightened the ranks around me. "No chance of taking a day or two breather before we dive back into weapon hunting?" Johann asked.

I was glad I wasn't the only one who wasn't crazy about this idea.

Tore shook his head. "They're trying to destroy the piece with eternal fire."

Greta gasped. A sea of somber faces filled my vision.

My stomach knotted into a pit. "What's eternal fire?" If it made everybody this unhappy, it had to be bad.

Huginn took to the skies and flew out of sight. Tore stared sadly at the note. And the rest of my protectors exchanged increasingly uncomfortable looks.

"Guys?" I repeated my question. "What's eternal fire?"

After a seeming eternity, the red-haired warrior stepped forward and gave me a small bow. "Goddess, I am Astrid. Leader of Vidar's army."

Whoa. Chick was in charge of all these firemen. *Girl power, for the win.*

"Nice to meet you, Astrid. What is eternal fire?" I asked for the third time. Because Astrid had stepped forward for a reason, right?

Her comrades shot her pitying looks as she moved closer to me and raised her shirt enough to reveal a nasty puckered scar. Her belly button had been consumed by thick, white, hardened skin. I bit down on my bottom lip to keep from gasping.

"My twin sister, Aria, was thrown into the eternal fire during a war on this very land." Astrid's voice was steady, but I sensed a deep sadness in her words.

I frowned, unsure of what to say.

"I was in Asgard, many realms away. When my sister's skin hit the eternal flame, my own skin roasted as if I was burning alive."

I brought my hand to my mouth. "I'm so sorry."

Astrid continued. "Eternal fire is comprised of the darkest energy in the cosmos. If anything can destroy Gud Morder, it would be that."

Tore looked up from his note to explain further. "The eternal flame moves continually. It's been spotted over lava pools on Muspelheim; then hours later, it shows up atop a mountain on Helheim. You can't predict where it will go. It is a possessed, dark energy that has no source and no keeper. We can't let your weapon anywhere near it. If even one piece of Gud Morder is destroyed, we won't be able to kill Nott. She's made herself so invincible, nothing but the complete sword will be able to destroy her. And if we don't destroy her, we'll never save Midgard, and we'll never wake your mom."

I let out a frustrated groan and kicked the dirt. "Then let's go get the next piece."

Nothing was going to get in the way of me healing my mother.

We gave Bodie and Greta a quick goodbye hug, and I asked Scarlet to fly them far enough away that they could Bifrost back to Canada.

'*Will find you,*' Scarlet told me.

I nodded. '*You better.*'

Astrid shot me a curious look as we trekked off to the pits from Huginn's note. "You're dragon bonded?" she asked.

"Apparently." I shrugged. Astrid continued to watch me with curiosity. "What?"

"Nothing." She picked up her pace, but I caught up to her.

"Not nothing. Tell me."

Astrid smiled. "When the Norns said that the person to defeat darkness would be a healer, well. We were all skeptical."

Ah. Now I understood. There must have been a slew of running jokes about me in Asgard. *How long until the healer fails?* They'd probably expected the task to go to a warrior, or even Revenge himself. I couldn't have been what anyone expected.

Astrid slowed down and turned her head to look at me. Since my protectors were up ahead, engaged in a heated discussion about the best way to drop in on the 'destroy Gud Morder party,' they didn't notice when Astrid leaned in and lowered her voice.

"When Vidar assigned me to aid you, I nearly refused. My talents are in high demand, and protecting a pointless cause seemed like a waste of my time. But when I walked into that tunnel and saw you fighting Nott with that blue whip, you earned my respect. And knowing that you are dragon bonded . . . well." She grinned and placed a hand on my shoulder. "It's an honor to fight beside you."

My throat got all tight, and my eyes filled with tears. I hadn't realized how much I needed to hear those words. I knew my four protectors believed in me, but to have the captain of Revenge's army tell me that I'd earned her respect meant everything.

I cleared my throat, trying to act tougher than I felt. "Thank you for standing with me."

Astrid nodded, and that was that. A weight had been lifted off my shoulders. I could do this. I could kill Nott.

I had to.

CHAPTER THIRTEEN

"**OKAY, WHO KNOWS THE** best way to kill a fire giant?" Astrid asked. The leader of Revenge's army had us tucked between a lava pit and a large outcropping of rocks, while she wrapped up the details of our attack.

"Uh," I floundered. My dragon nudged my hand with her head, and I reached up to pet her. A peace had washed over me the minute Scarlet had returned from dropping Bodie and Greta off at the Bifrost site. I'd joked about her being my pet, but already our bond went much deeper than that. Saving her life had bound us in a way I'd never thought possible. She was my family, the same way my protectors were, and I knew she'd do anything for me. It was humbling. And just the hugest bit awesome.

"*Hei*? Fire giant elimination, anyone?" Astrid repeated her question.

Tore looked up. "I decapitated one once. Worked pretty well."

Astrid nodded. "Correct. A simple blade to the groin will drop a fire giant like a whining baby. Then you can slice their head off."

Despite the talk of beheading, Mack, Tore, and Johann all covered their man-parts.

"That's awful," Mack whispered. His face was contorted in pain, even though no one had actually touched him.

Astrid grinned. "I'm not here to make friends, boys. When I fight, I fight dirty."

Okay, Astrid was officially my girl crush.

Johann's eyes turned a molten grey as he looked Astrid up and down with intense longing. If things weren't so dire, I'd have teased him. Instead, I made a mental note to heckle Hannie later and focused my attention on the task at hand.

Blade to the groin. Slice off the head. Got it.

One of the hottie firefighters stepped forward and held up one hand. "We must warn you. If even one lick of the eternal fire touches your skin . . ."

He let the open-ended sentence hang in the air. Message received. Stay away from all things hot and glowing.

I turned to address the group. "If Nott shows up again, feel free to kick her into the fire and end all of this."

"Agreed." Astrid nodded. "Regulation weapons won't kill Nott, but nobody's ever tried eternal fire. It's worth a shot." Then she withdrew her blade. The nearby lava pit glinted red off the steel. She knelt on one knee, her head lowered in prayer. Her warriors did the same, and my protectors and I followed suit. I wasn't sure what we were doing, but after seeing the way she commanded her team, I was fairly positive I'd follow Astrid anywhere.

I knew for sure that Johann would.

"*Må vi hedre sjelene til Valhalla,*" Astrid vowed.

"*Må vi hedre sjelene til Valhalla,*" her warriors repeated.

I furrowed my brow. When this was over, I was *so* signing up for language classes. Tore leaned over and translated, "May we honor the souls of Valhalla."

"Thanks," I whispered.

"*Velkommen,*" he whispered back.

The warriors rose in unison, their pleasant demeanors gone. *Way* gone. Hardened faces and clenched jaws met my gaze, and I knew they were ready to fight to the death. *Skit* just got real.

Astrid walked over to place a hand on my shoulder. "Fly safe, warrior-sister. We'll have your back."

She dropped her hand to her neck and fingered the feather charm of her necklace. For a split second, I thought I caught a glimpse of fear in her eyes. But as quickly as it may have come, it was gone. I felt for Astrid—I couldn't imagine her pain at confronting the thing that killed her twin sister and literally scarred her for life. But, ever the warrior, she simply turned away and readied her hand on her blade.

'We fly over fire now?' Scarlet nudged my leg.

I nodded to her and stroked the red scales between her eyes. The act was soothing for both of us. Astrid believed the best plan was a distraction, so Scarlet and I were staging an air assault in order to get our ground crew in. Tore approved of the idea because it kept me out of the fight and safe in the skies. I approved of the idea because I knew I could tell Scarlet to swoop in and pick Tore up if, God forbid, things went south.

Please, things, don't go south.

Tore stepped closer to me, eating up the space between us and drawing me in for a deliciously wicked kiss. "Bora Bora," he whispered as he withdrew his lips from mine.

"Clothing optional," I replied. With a wink, I swung one leg over Scarlet and mentally prepared to fly over a group of angry fire giants and a flame so powerful it could travel across realms to burn the belly button off the toughest chick I'd ever met.

No big deal.

Once I was positioned behind Scarlet's wings, I gave her the command, and we shot into the air. With one last look at the warriors who were supposed to take on a dozen fire giants and one lethal flame, I flared the Liv to life in my hand. I was tired, I was hungry, and I was about to pass out from dehydration. But nothing would stop me from saving my mother, from having the chance to have a relationship with her. And nothing would stop me from helping all of the humans who didn't even know that they depended on me. I wouldn't let them down.

Scarlet flew higher, and when we emerged over the rocks, I gasped. A sea of menacing fire giants stood like sentinels around the top of a small peak. At the tip of that peak was a neon-green flame. The Eternal Fire.

'Stay away from that flame,' I told Scarlet.

She chuffed. *'Obvious.'*

I snapped my head back in shock. *'Did you just say obvious? Was that sarcasm?'* Scarlet was *so* my dragon.

She gave a slight nod and began to circle the giants.

Fun time was over. Now we had to put Astrid's plan into effect.

Focusing my thoughts on the Liv pulsing in my palm, I molded my whip into shape and cracked it as hard as I could. It boomed, causing the fire giants to look up.

"Where's my weapon?" I roared. My goal was to keep their attention on the sky, so my protectors and our warrior crew could get into position. My team moved below me, but I kept my eyes on the giants, not wanting to draw any attention to the ground team.

"It's the girl!" One of the giants raised his fist trying to reach for me. It shouldn't have come as a surprise that he could talk—I was riding a telepathic dragon, after all. But still . . . *Whoa.*

'Go lower!' I instructed Scarlet. She wound us downward, making small circles over the massive beasts.

When we were ten feet above one of the giants' heads, I cracked my whip again. The action relieved the beast of one of his ears. His face crumpled into a ball of rage as he let out a roar. With surprising agility, he jumped high into the air, taking hold of Scarlet's tail in his gnarled fist.

"No!" I screamed. I spun on her back, ready to take the giant's hand clean off. But just as he yanked her tail, Tore came out of nowhere and rammed his blade right into the giant's crotch. The giant's stubby fingers released Scarlet's tail, and then we were skyward again.

'*Sorry, girl,*' I told her.

'*Not your fault,*' she responded.

Her forgiveness didn't lessen my regret, but I didn't have time to berate myself. The battle had officially begun. The warriors had started their attack, and now it was my job to find the piece of my weapon. I allowed my eyes to settle as I scanned the energy of the area. The eternal fire was so thick, it was hard to see anything else— even with my energy sight. When a glint of light finally caught my eye, I yelped with joy. There, just on the ledge of the small peak, was a piece of Gud Morder. It glowed fiercely from its perch between two rocks. I told Scarlet where we needed to go, then held on for dear life as she nose-dived toward the light.

'*I'm going to jump off. When I have the piece, I want you to swing back around and pick me up again,*' I told her.

'*Yes, Master Allie.*'

When Scarlet got me within a few feet of the ground, I swung my legs onto her back and got into a crouch. Then I leapt forward, landing on the rocks with a hard jolt. A wave of pain shot from my ankles to my shins, and I fought valiantly to get my bearings. Death by eternal flame was *so* not on my agenda today. *Or ever.*

When my equilibrium was restored, I chanced a look to my left. A few feet away, Astrid was engaged in a fierce battle with one of the giants. She jammed her blade into his groin and kicked out with her leg, pushing him backward into the fire. A horrible hissing noise rose up, and a searing pop resounded as the eternal flame eviscerated the giant's body. Astrid turned her attention to the next giant, and I refocused on the light that shone near my feet. Taking care not to make any sudden movements that might draw attention to my presence, I knelt down and shoved my hand between the rocks. I pushed my fingers through the tight crevice, reaching until I touched the twin blades. *Gotcha!*

As I stood up, I realized that I'd sent my waist pouch back to the safe house. *Stupid.* I was afraid the piece might fall out of my pockets, so I kept it clutched in my hand, tucked tight against my stomach while I waited for my ride. The crimson wings of my dragon flapped down from the sky, but as I bent to leap onto her back, a black blur passed before my eyes. Taloned fingers wrapped around my throat, and before I knew what was happening, Nott herself was hauling me across the rocks and toward the fire. For a frail looking woman, she was strong as all get out. My feet kicked out as I struggled against Nott's hold, all the while fighting to breathe.

'*Look out!*' Scarlet's warning came too late. Nott threw me across the back of a black dragon and flew us over the eternal flame. My body was bent awkwardly across the creature, with my cheek pressed to its neck and my legs dangling precariously over one side of its torso. I had no grip whatsoever; Nott's hand at my throat was the only thing preventing me from falling off. The pressure on my windpipe was unbearable, and I struggled valiantly to stabilize myself. I kept my arm pinned to my chest, hiding the weapon piece from Nott's view, but my protection wouldn't matter if Nott released her hold on my throat. The piece—and my body—would be destroyed on contact if she dropped us into that flame.

Which, it seemed, she was hell-bent on doing. She had no reason to keep me alive.

Nott bent low to speak into my ear. Her hot breath washed over my skin, its acidic odor making me gag. "You know, after I shattered Gud Morder, I realized that I couldn't touch the pieces. The weapon had locked itself down—some kind of a failsafe conceived by its insipid creators. Over time, it became clear that only you could retrieve its pieces."

"Allie!" Tore's voice boomed from the ground.

Nott loosened her hold on my throat, but not by much. Black spots had begun to dance across my vision, and the heat of the eternal flame was dancing upward, lapping closer to my skin. *Oh, God.*

The black spots gave way to a streak of red, and my body was wrenched by a mighty jolt. I blinked through the haze that had become my vision, to see Scarlet whipping her barbed tail at the black dragon's stomach. The dragon shrieked with each spiky strike, but Nott didn't seem to be fazed. Instead, she studied the eternal fire with lust in her eyes. In that moment, I knew with absolute certainty that she was going to chuck me in. I was going to die.

And I knew, with absolute certainty, that I was going to fight that fate with every ounce of will I had left.

"In all my life," Nott waxed, "I've never seen the eternal flame close up. How fortunate that it appeared when it did. The Norns must want you and that weapon destroyed, so that I can rule Midgard."

Her hand loosened just enough for me to gulp in a huge lungful of air. I pinned her with a murderous look and choked out, "Burn in hell, Nott."

It was kill or be killed, and my morning yoga sessions with Mack were about to pay off. With one big kick, I swung my legs up toward my head and straddled the dragon's neck. The movement left Nott with two choices—let go of my throat or try to keep her hold on me with one broken arm. As expected, she chose the former, and I took advantage of her shift to whip my arm up and fist her long, black hair. I wrenched her head to the side, forcing her off the dragon. Without an ounce of remorse, I released my grip, sending Nott tumbling toward the eternal flame. I quickly brought my hand back to grip the dragon's neck. Since my other hand still clutched the piece of Gud Morder, I struggled to maintain my one-handed hold on the dragon's slippery scales, while riding backwards over a god-killing fire. I scooted forward, closer to the dragon's wings, and looked down. I was about to witness the end of Nott's reign—her body was feet away from being consumed by the realms' deadliest blaze. But a second before she hit the flame, Nott's body transformed into that stupid flock of birds. They scattered, soaring through the sky and avoiding the flames completely.

"No!" I shouted. In my distraction, I didn't realize the dragon was shaking me off. He jerked his neck, and I slipped, losing my grip and falling fast. Time slowed to a crawl as I clawed at the empty air around me. The heat of the sickly green flames lapped closer to my legs, and I sensed each swirl, each agonizingly slow burst of fire that surged closer to my body. Scarlet careened through the sky, her panic evident in the frantic flaps of her wings. But she was too far away to save me. I was done for. Gud Morder and I would die together, and all hope for my mother and my beloved Midgard would be lost.

Surprisingly it wasn't either of those things that bothered me the most. In those final seconds, which seemed to stretch into minutes, it was the thought of leaving the blond-haired demigod with piercing blue eyes that broke my heart. Tore screamed my name from just beyond the flame's reach, his arms restrained by Johann and Astrid. He fought valiantly, seemingly ready to leap into the eternal fire to save me. *Tore.* He was the one I would miss the most, the one I would regret not getting more time with. He was my first love—the one who'd owned my heart, without my even knowing it, from the moment I'd laid into him with my pink can of pepper spray. He had become my world, and now we were going to be lost to each other, forever.

I closed my eyes as the heat came closer; I was afraid to watch as my body was eviscerated. I wanted my death to be over quickly; hopefully I wouldn't suffer for long. *Goodbye protectors. Greta. Mom. Tore.* Grief wracked my heart as I thought of my love, and an agonizing cry tore from my lungs. I wrapped my arms around my ribcage and tucked my knees to my chest, giving in to the pain of losing Tore and my family more than the pain of losing my life. With one final surge, the heat lapped at my feet before vanishing completely. Instead of the quick death I'd hoped for, my body slammed into the earth like a sack of flour. And instead of immediate evisceration, my ankles snapped and pain shot up my legs. The rest of my body came down hard on my right side, landing not on a god-killing fire, but atop the rocky peak where the fire had just been.

The eternal flame had vanished. I was still alive. But the agony wracking my body very nearly made me wish I wasn't. I'd never felt pain like this before in my life. A wave of nausea rolled through me, and I turned my head to the side to throw up. My legs burned as if they'd been shattered, and my elbow seared with such intensity I feared I would pass out.

"Scarlet!" Tore's voice sounded as if it was nearby. I vomited again before I felt his steady arms scoop me up. "You're okay, Allie. You're gonna be okay." He wasn't very convincing—his voice shook, and his face was lined with tension. The pain was too overwhelming to manage, and I found myself fighting to stay conscious. One side of my ribcage had to be broken; my ankles were definitely shattered, and there was a strong possibility I didn't even have an elbow anymore.

"The eternal flame," I rasped. "What happened?"

Astrid's face came into view over Tore's shoulder. "Right before you hit the flames, they snuffed out. Blessed be."

"It must have been the Norns. They're protecting Allie until she can fulfill her purpose." Mack's deep voice came from behind my head.

I wanted to reply, say something witty about my protectors being out of a job, but a black curtain was closing over my eyelids. I might have been a demigod, but the pain was too much to bear.

I closed my eyes and drifted peacefully away.

****

The incessantly cheerful songbird trilling just outside my consciousness was one eight-count away from getting a shoe thrown at it. Or something much worse if I was strong enough to get the Liv up and running. My sleep had been fitful and, as far as I was concerned, all too brief. But the bird didn't care that the girl tasked with saving the realms from a demonic monster needed her rest. The only thing it seemed to care about was finishing its unbelievably long, and unbelievably high pitched, tune.

Stupid songbird.

"Argh." I raised my hands, intending to press them against my temples to stop the pounding within my skull. But the movement brought on a whole new surge of pain, this time a sharp stabbing along my sternum. The bones creaked in protest before letting loose with a rapid-fire series of daggers to my chest. *What happened to me?*

"Try not to move, Allie." Tore's voice was close. I forced my eyelids open, and in a moment of *déjà vu*, I realized my favorite protector was settled in the same chair he'd claimed the last time I'd been benched in Asgard's healing unit. Which must have meant . . .

"Crap," I groaned. "I'm back in the hospital, aren't I?"

"That's a good thing." Tore leaned forward to brush the hair out of my face. He let his fingertips linger on my forehead when he said, "It means you made it out of Muspelheim alive."

"Told you Nott had nothing on me and my dragon." I tried to laugh, but my ribs screamed out in protest. Instead, I settled for staring into Tore's endless eyes. "I'm sorry I let her get away."

"Are you kidding me? You did more than any of us could have. You stopped the eternal flame. Nobody's ever done that before—not that we're aware of, anyway."

"Thanks," I whispered. I turned my head to the side so Tore's fingertips slid to my temple. "Do you think you could rub my head? It hurts like a mother."

"Of course." Tore gently massaged the pounding skin with one hand and raised the other to speak into his wrist communicator. "Greta, get pain antidotes in here right away."

"Thanks," I whispered again. Tore's magical fingers coaxed the worst of the headache from my body, but the second he broke contact, the pain would return with a vengeance. Either I was severely dehydrated from our recent trip to the fiery realm, or Nott and her minions had done a number on me physically. In all likelihood, I probably suffered from a combination of both. "Do I have any broken bones? Besides whatever's happening with my chest?"

"Your sternum's cracked," Tore confirmed. "You shattered your tibia, a few bones in each of your feet, and did a number to your kneecap. Oh, and your elbow. Fifteen breaks total."

"Ugh," I groaned. That was a *lot* of damage. "How long am I going to be in here this time?"

"Not long, if I can help it." Greta breezed into the room, carrying a single tray laden with vials and crystals. She placed the tray on the table by the window, then slid the glass pane up to let in fresh air. I groaned as the bird's song increased in volume, and my healer friend gently shooed the creature from its windowsill perch.

"Thank you," I muttered. "He was getting on my last nerve."

"Mine too," Greta laughed. She tossed her long hair over her shoulder. The loose waves were framed by a single braid that crowned her hair, making her look every bit the Asgardian. "I'm guessing you have a pretty bad headache after everything you went through. And I'm guessing our little bird friend was not helping."

"You guessed right," I agreed.

"Well, let's do something about that." Greta turned her attention to the tray, where she began mixing vials into a small cup. Her white tunic fluttered as a light breeze came through the window. The whole effect was extremely soothing. Or it would be, once the knives in my skull cut me a break. Tore's head rub was no longer having its desired effect. *Hurry up with the pain meds already. I mean, Namaste, headache.*

Greta turned around and moved to my side. She held out the small glass. "Drink this," she offered. "It's a blend of herbs and crystal extracts that should expedite your healing. Plus, I put a little something in there for your pain management."

"Bless you, Greta." I looked to Tore for support. "Help me up? Gently?" If I drank this thing lying down, it would end up all over me.

"Of course." Tore placed one hand behind my shoulder blades and slid the other behind my lower back. "On three. One. Two."

"Three. Oh my God it hurts!" A thousand blades unleashed themselves on my torso. I tried not to sob as Tore carefully lifted me high enough that I could drink. Greta placed the glass to my lips, and I downed its contents in four painful swallows. By the time Tore returned me back to the mattress, my chest had stopped trying to kill me. And my headache had dropped to near-manageable levels. Whatever Greta had put in that cup, it was some good stuff.

"Next time, we use a bendy straw so I don't have to move," I groaned. "You guys have those in Asgard, right?"

"No," Greta and Tore said together.

"But we'll have some brought in," Greta hastened to add when I shot her a lethal glare.

"Good idea," I muttered. My poor friends and their bendy-straw-free childhoods. No wonder Tore grew up to be such a grump.

Said grump bent over to brush my forehead with his lips. "You're doing great. And when you're ready, there's somebody here who wants to see you."

I arched one eyebrow. "Tell Bodie he can thank me for saving his butt by taking over my next four shifts on Mack's chore chart."

"Funny." Tore chuckled. "But I was talking about Elora."

"Oh, my gosh, send her in!" I urged.

"Don't you want to recover a bit first?" Tore asked.

"Actually . . . I'm already starting to feel better. Jeez, Greta, what did you put in that cup?" It was amazing how quickly the magic crystal pain medicine was working.

"You don't have to ask me twice. *Hei hei,* goddaughter." My light-elf godmother glided into the room. She carried a cake in one hand and an armful of brightly colored blooms in the other.

My bad mood instantly vanished. It was impossible to be upset around cake, flowers, and Mack's mom. Although I had only known Elora for a short time, her presence both strengthened and comforted me. Being near her was like having a piece of my own mom back.

"Oh, sweetheart." Elora clucked her tongue as she approached my bedside. "You must be in so much pain."

"I've felt better," I admitted. My gaze slid over to Tore, who raised one eyebrow in question. When I waved for him to help me up again, he slid his hand behind my back and gently guided me to a seated position. I only winced once; if Greta could bottle that healing juice, she'd make a killing on the black market.

"I thought I told you to take care of her," Elora admonished Tore.

"I failed," Tore admitted. "Nott met us at the eternal fire and—"

"Nott?" Greta gasped at the same time Elora sucked in a sharp breath. When Tore brought me to the healing unit, he must have forgotten to mention Nott's involvement in my injuries to Greta.

"Eternal fire?" Elora asked. "Allie, you couldn't have touched it or you'd be . . ."

"Dead? Yeah. Wished I was for a few minutes there. No, the flame fizzled out right before I fell in. Then Tore got me out, and," I shrugged, "here we are."

"But how?" Elora set the cake and flowers down beside Greta's healing tray and stood at the foot of my bed. "Never mind, you've been through enough. Oh, you poor, sweet thing. And shame on you, Tore Vidarsson." She shot Tore a disappointed look. "Next time, you leave my goddaughter someplace safe before you even think about doing something so dangerous as approaching Nott, or the eternal fire, without Gud Morder."

A rumble of laughter built in Tore's throat. "Mrs. Medisjon, if you can convince Allie to stay behind, I will one hundred percent support your decision. But she's come a long way from the frail human who once needed pepper spray to take down her attackers."

I was *so* never living that down.

"I'm not staying anywhere," I said. "Not until we wake my mom."

"And speaking of." Elora glanced at the flowers and cake with a smile.

"Ooh, are those for me? I miss cake." I eyed the table hungrily. I was long overdue for a good piece of cake. Or seven. My appetite had returned in full force—I was definitely feeling better.

"One of the bouquets is for you." Elora's gentle features turned up in a smile. "The other, and the cake, is for your mom."

"My mom's awake?" I blurted. I threw the covers to the side and was halfway off the bed before I realized my bottom half wasn't as healed as I thought it was. My kneecaps groaned with the weight of swinging legs, and I dropped back onto the bed. "Ow."

Tore gently cupped my bare calves in his massive hands and shifted them back onto the bed. I really needed to speak with someone about the healing-unit-issued attire. A few more inches of fabric on the gowns wouldn't have killed anyone. But they would have saved me from nearly flashing my godmother. And my hot-as-all-get-out boyfriend. This was totally not the way I wanted him to see me naked for the first time. I mean, *really*.

"Easy, Pepper." Tore pulled the blanket over my legs, evading my mortification. "Your mom's still asleep. She's just down the hall. We can visit her once your bones re-fuse."

My heart plummeted. Of course my mom wasn't awake—we still had three more pieces of Gud Morder to retrieve before we could heal the weapon, kill Nott, and free her from her curse. *Stupid curse.* "Right," I mumbled. "Wait, you bring cake to a sleeping person?"

"I do every year on her birthday." Elora gave a sanguine smile.

My jaw dropped to my still-sore sternum. *Shut the door, it's my mom's birthday?*

Tore tucked my blanket back over my legs before lacing his fingers through mine. "You're turning white. You okay?"

"Yeah, I just . . . I didn't even know when her birthday was. Gran didn't talk about her a lot—I guess that was to keep me safe. But . . ." My voice dropped to a whisper. "I've never celebrated her birthday with her before."

Oh, my God. Do I really get to do this?

"You celebrated with her when you were very little," Elora said gently. "Before Nott's curse. I was there. Tore, your mom was there, too."

Tore stiffened at my side. I gave his fingers a squeeze, sending a silent 'got your back, boyfriend,' that I hoped he picked up on.

"Your grandmother made a beautiful chocolate cake, Allie. And every year since, I've made that same recipe and brought it to your mother's bedside. I thought if you were up to it today, you could bring it to her with me." Elora smiled softly, letting me know the choice was mine to make. Did I want to celebrate my mom's birthday with her for the first time ever—that I could remember, at least?

Hell yeah, I did.

"Hey, Greta?" I asked.

My friend stepped forward from the window, where she'd been stationed since Elora entered. "Yes?"

"Do they have wheelchairs in Asgard?"

Greta actually laughed at that, straight up laughed at me. "Of course we do. Why wouldn't we?"

"You don't have bendy straws, but you do have—never mind." I shook my head. "Can I get one? I want to go see my mom."

Greta bit her bottom lip. "You should probably give yourself another hour or two to let the elixirs take effect."

"Nope, I'm good." I guided my feet to the side of the bed, biting down hard on the inside of my cheek as I lowered them over the edge. Thankfully, the pain that filled my legs was slightly less unmanageable than it had been the last time. "See? Wheelchair, please."

"Oh, Allie." Greta sighed in resignation, then ducked into the hallway. She returned a moment later with a device that almost looked like a Midgardian wheelchair. Almost. It hovered over the ground, emitting a blue light and a soft hum. It didn't have wheels, but it did have handles. It also had a small knob on one of the arm rests that I assumed let its occupant steer for herself. *Cool.*

"You going to jump into that chair, or are you going to let me help you?" Tore watched my wiggling butt with barely-contained amusement.

"You may help me," I acquiesced.

Tore wrapped me in his thick arms and lifted me into the high-tech roving device with more care than I could have imagined back when I thought he was a creepy park attacker. Then he took the blanket from the foot of my bed and tucked it around my bare shins. I was used to him flinging me around in the complex or sparring with me in the woods behind the safe house, so this moment was kind of surreal. Gentle, caretaker Tore was all kinds of foreign, and all kinds of adorable.

"So, I take it you'd like to sing 'Happy Birthday' with me?" Elora winked.

"You betcha." I grinned. "Tore, you know how to drive one of these?"

With a chuckle, Tore took hold of the chair's handles and guided me out the door. When Elora emerged with the cake and flowers, we followed her down the hall. Tore placed one hand on my shoulder as I drew a nervous breath.

"You okay?" he asked.

"Yes. No. Both," I admitted. On the one hand, I was badly battered and my mom was trapped in a curse. On the other hand, neither of us was dead, and I was about to celebrate her birthday with her, in person. My feelings were all kinds of mixed up.

Tore bent down so his lips brushed my ear. "I understand," was all he said. And it was enough. Tore was with me, and knowing that single fact made everything else disappear. We'd get through this—and everything else the universe threw at us—together. Because we were a team. Because we fought to right the wrongs of the darkest side of evil. And because, underneath it all, Tore really did understand.

And that was all I needed.

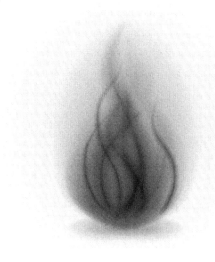

CHAPTER FOURTEEN

WE ENTERED MY MOM'S room in a funny little parade. Elora led the way with the cake; Tore followed behind, pushing my wheelchair; and Greta begrudgingly brought up the rear, muttering the whole time about how I was only hurting my own healing if I didn't take the time to mend. When I craned my head around Elora to see my mom, my breath caught in my throat. There were hundreds of bouquets, gifts, and cards scattered around my mom's room. Greta had to sneak past us and move some of them out into the hall so that there was room to roll my chair beside my mom. Elora and I flanked her bedside, while Tore stood behind me with a hand on my shoulder. Greta left us alone, closing the door behind her to give us privacy.

My mom looked better than she had the last time I'd seen her here. She didn't have any crazy, evil, dark energy cords, just the usual blobs that held her in her curse. Her face looked so peaceful, lips in a relaxed almost-smile. It gave me some degree of comfort to know she wasn't suffering.

"Your daughter is getting into quite the trouble over here, Eir," Elora smiled as she reached over to grasp my mom's hand.

I grinned. "Not on purpose. It's not my fault danger follows me."

With Elora here, talking like this, it was almost as if my mom was awake and we were all just joking around.

But just as quickly as Elora's bright smile lit up her face, it fell into a frown. "Another birthday like this." Tears lined her eyes, and she bit down on her bottom lip. I leaned forward in my wheelchair and grasped Elora's hand, setting it atop my mother's.

"Tell me a story about her. Please. I have no stories," I begged my godmother.

Her face shifted immediately. "One does come to mind, but she would kill me for telling you."

I rolled my eyes. "She's asleep. It will be our secret."

Elora's eyes crinkled as her smile turned into a full-blown laugh. "Tore, this story involves your dad as well."

"Great." Tore muttered from somewhere over my shoulder.

Elora leaned forward, her entire demeanor changing. "Well the demigods, gods, and those of us with extraordinary affinities go to a special school. I was permitted to go for four years once it was clear I had a strong affinity with the healing arts and midwifery."

Interesting. I didn't know demigods went to fancy schools. Why had I been shipped off to human high school with all the mean girls?

Elora smiled again, "Now, grade eight isn't a nice time for any girl. When your mom was that age, she hadn't yet grown into her radiant beauty."

Preach. I was *still* trying to block out middle school and the horrors that happened there.

"Your mom carried a bit of extra weight, her hair was rather unruly, and her teeth . . . well, let's just say she was a late bloomer."

Tore chuckled behind me, and I grinned. I liked this story. It was hard to believe the supermodel on the bed in front of me had ever had an awkward phase.

"The winter ball was approaching," Elora continued, "and no one had asked your mom yet. Vidar, being the god that he is, took it upon himself to make flyers offering one hundred gold coins for anyone that would take poor Eir to the dance."

Tore's hand clenched my shoulder so hard I squealed.

"Sorry," he muttered. I reached up to give his hand a light squeeze.

Elora waved her hand at our reaction. "Adolescents can be mean no matter what realm they live on."

"What did my mom do? Did anyone ask her to the dance?" This story had better have a happy ending.

Elora looked at my mom with an adoring gaze and continued. "I'd never seen Eir so mad. Not in all my life. It was that day, on the school yard, that the Liv awakened within her. Tore, you know how much your father values his hair, right?"

Tore cleared his throat. "He loves his hair more than he ever loved me."

Elora nodded. "Well, Eir pinned him against the wall, fashioned a sickle from the Liv and buzzed his hair clean off. He was completely and totally bald."

Laughter burst from my throat. "She didn't!"

Elora laughed along with me. "She most certainly did. But being Eir, she felt bad and went back the night before the dance to use her healing powers to grow his hair back."

Tore groaned. "He didn't deserve it."

Elora smiled. "But that's Eir."

I couldn't stop grinning. It was a good story, exactly the story I needed to hear. It gave me a glimpse into my mom's life.

"Did she go to the dance?" I asked.

Elora nodded. "With your father, Allie."

My heart pinched. I wished so much that I could have met him. My eyes moved to my mom, and I could have sworn a tiny smile lit up her face.

"Happy birthday, Mom. You need to wake up so you can teach me how to shave Tore's head with the Liv when he gets out of line."

"Hold up, Pepper, that's not nice," Tore admonished. "Besides, I never get out of line. I'm perfect."

"Keep on telling yourself that." I snorted.

We spent the next hour chatting around my mom, telling her stories as if she was fully conscious. We laughed, cried, and ate cake. It was wonderful and just what I needed after my deeply scarring Nott experience.

After a while, a soft knock sounded at the door, and Greta poked her head in. "Allie, I need to check your vitals."

I nodded to my friend and looked back at my mother. I'd needed this family time badly—no matter how brief it had been, it had grounded my soul. "I'm gonna get you out of here, Mom. Hang tight."

Elora leaned over to kiss my mom's cheek. "No more birthdays like this. I want to hear your laugh again, my dear friend."

With tears glistening on my cheeks, I allowed Tore to push my chair back into my room. My body was in substantially less pain; it felt merely bruised instead of shattered. Demigod healing rocked.

Once inside my room, I let Greta fuss over me. She poked and prodded for several minutes before finally nodding. "I think you'll be able to walk with an aid for a few hours, and after that you should be good as new."

She stepped into the hallway for a moment and came back carrying a cane. I ran my gaze from the elongated crystal bulb at the top, down the rich, mahogany staff. "That's a cool cane. I mean, if a girl needed a cane, then that would be the cane to have."

Greta smiled. "The crystal will accelerate your healing."

"So, she's all good?" Tore seemed to be unsure.

Greta smiled. "She's all good. What's next?"

Tore reached over to lace his fingers through mine. "Now, we fuse Gud Morder."

I nodded. "What are we waiting for?"

There was no such thing as down time when an evil goddess was gunning for control of the realms. All I could do was keep moving forward.

And, of course, dream of Bora Bora.

****

I kept a tight grip on my cane as I hobbled into the house. The enthusiastic barking that greeted me reminded me that we'd recently acquired a dog—one I'd completely and totally forgotten about. Killer bounded over to Tore and me with his endless enthusiasm. He looked like he was going to jump straight on top of me, which would undoubtedly lead to a fresh wave of broken bones. I winced, but Tore stepped in front of me and folded his arms across his chest.

"Killer, heel!" Tore commanded. Killer skidded to a stop, panting wildly. Tore leaned down to run a hand behind his ears. "Good boy."

"Sorry." Johann raced into the hallway. "I had him tied up but, well, he's strong. Welcome home, Allie."

"Thanks." I accepted Johann's fist bump before limping into the living room. I cast my gaze around the space, moving from the spot by the couch where Mel packed crystal wands into a bag, over to the fireplace where Mack was deep in conversation with a tall brunette.

"Ahem," I cleared my throat with a smile.

"Allie!" Mack's face lit up when he saw me. He crossed to my side and enveloped me in the gentlest of hugs. A quick scan of his energy revealed that his heart center radiated love. But as happy as he looked to see me, I was pretty sure that glow wasn't for me.

Finally.

The brunette stepped forward and bowed lightly to me. "Namaste, Allie. I'm so glad to hear you're healing."

I chuckled to myself. This chick was perfect for Mack.

"Er, Namaste. And thank you."

The smattering of freckles along her nose crinkled with her smile. Her long, brown hair was draped over one gently-muscled shoulder, and she radiated a peaceful vibe that immediately put me at ease. This girl had amazingly pure energy. She was another good egg.

"I'm Lela," the girl introduced herself.

Mel popped up beside me. "She's my master healing teacher. I'm going to work in the healing unit when I'm older. Like Greta."

I smiled at Mel. "And you'll be amazing there."

Lela clasped Mack's hands lightly in farewell. "It was lovely to meet you, Mack."

When their hands touched, sparks of pure pink energy shot from their bodies.

Lela swallowed hard before turning to face me. "Bless you on your journey." She folded her hands together and nodded her head. Then she and Mel were on their way.

Mack just stood, his eyes locked intently on the closed door, as the light of the Bifrost flashed through the windows. "I'm going to marry that girl," he vowed.

A raucous laugh ripped from Tore's throat as he clapped Mack on the back. "The eternal romantic. When he falls, he falls hard."

Johann, who'd been clearing the room of chewed up Killer sticks, joined in Tore's laughter. "Dude, you've known her a couple hours."

Mack shrugged. "You'll see."

"Don't ever change, Mack," I begged. "You're perfect just the way you are."

Mack raised his chin "Thank you, Allie. It's a blessing to see you healing. You gave us quite the fright, falling into the eternal fire."

I nodded. "You and me, both."

Tore looked around. "Where's Bodie? And Greta?"

It had taken me longer than I wanted to convince the upper echelon of the healing unit that I was sufficiently recovered to leave Asgard. While Tore and I had bartered for my freedom, Greta had returned to Vancouver ahead of us. She needed the time to prepare for the Gud Morder binding session.

"Guys?" I raised my eyebrow. "Where are they?"

Johann's mouth pulled up in a devilish grin. "Probably in Bodie's room. You know, getting reacquainted."

Mack just shook his head.

My mouth popped open. "Wait. What? Tell me everything!"

Johann eagerly stepped closer to me. "After we dropped you off in Asgard, we came back to see how he was doing. We found them together, making out on the couch."

"Johann! Have some discretion," Mack scolded. But I just grinned from ear-to-ear. Bodie finally got to right the wrong of that kiss. Sometimes karma got things just right.

Killer barked then. Johann and I jumped apart, while Mack groaned. "He eats as much as a small horse, Tore."

Tore looked proudly at Killer and walked to the kitchen to get his food. "Wait until Allie's dragon moves in. Then you're *really* going to have a mess on your hands."

Mack shuddered.

While I tried to picture my tidy protector and my oversized dragon cohabitating, Bodie and Greta came down the stairs. Their hands were entwined, and they both had swollen lips and mussed-up hair.

"Hey, guys. What's up?" Bodie asked.

Johann wagged his eyebrows. "That's what she said." His comment elicited a groan from Greta.

"Really, Johann?" she chided.

"We owe him about a thousand of those," I pointed out. "Sorry, it's payback time."

Greta shook her head. "I suppose." She met my eyes, and we both broke into ear-to-ear grins. I'd learned that life was all about timing. And this was Bodie and Greta's time. I wished them nothing but the best—they deserved it.

Tore walked out of the kitchen with a set jaw and a steady gaze. Suddenly, he was all business.

"Bodie, retrieve the weapon pieces. Mack and Johann, secure the complex. Greta, do . . . whatever it is you do. Allie, come with me." We hadn't been in Vancouver for fifteen whole minutes, and Tore was back to barking orders.

Typical, adorable Tore.

"On it." Johann hightailed it out the back door, with Mack and Greta hot on his heels. Bodie ducked up the stairs, his footsteps overhead letting me know he was *en route* to the safe.

"Do they always do what you tell them?" I followed Tore into the kitchen, set my cane on the countertop, and leaned my elbows on the island.

"When they know what's good for them, they do." Tore shrugged. "You'd be wise to do the same."

I treated him to my best eye roll. "Dream on, Protector."

Tore chuckled. "Come on. Let's get you suited up." He tilted his head at the kitchen table, where it looked like Greta had already set out my armor. She'd sent it home with Mack while I was still in the healing unit. If it's fresh sheen was any indication, Mack had taken it upon himself to give it a nice polish while I'd been in recovery. Bless.

"Any word on Nott?" I asked as I limped to the table. I picked up my extra-shiny arm piece and positioned it over my left shoulder.

"Not officially." Tore came up behind me. His fingers brushed the bare skin of my arm as he strapped the shoulder piece into place. "But if the earthquake in Southern California is any indication, she's not happy. A freeway near downtown LA collapsed before sunrise this morning. Twenty people were killed."

I sucked in a sharp breath. "Twenty people? My God."

"There's more." Tore gave the strap another tug, then handed me my wrist cuff. "The quake cut power to most of downtown, and one of the local gangs figured it was the perfect opportunity to loot the shops. A few of the owners happened to be in early, and they decided to fight back."

"How many casualties?" I whispered.

"A lot." Tore grimaced. "Humans are innately reactive. But those shop owners had to know they weren't going to be strong enough to take on an entire gang. If they'd sought out law enforcement, or rallied their community . . ."

"There probably wasn't time for that kind of planning in the moment," I offered gently. Unlike Tore, I'd had the experience of living as a human firsthand. I could only imagine how terrified those owners must have been when looters busted into their shops, whereas Tore would have grown up with the luxury of going all demigod on their butts and killing them with one well-aimed broadsword.

"True. But lack of cohesion is a big-picture problem, and it's why Nott has been so successful at driving her stake into this planet." Tore strapped the cuff to my wrist. "Many humans, for whatever reason, are reluctant to believe the best in each other. It shows in the way they treat opposing religions, political parties, Hel, even the way they treat total strangers on their internet."

Whoa. I'd stumbled into a whole new subject that got Tore all hot and bothered. "Not everyone's that way," I countered. "There are a lot of good-hearted humans, who believe in happy ever after and want to see each other succeed."

"True. And those humans are the reason their race has survived as long as it has. But they are not the vocal majority." Tore continued, "Nott didn't invent the race wars, or the class wars, or any of the negativity that plagues Midgard. But some humans' willingness to embrace negative thought patterns, to turn on those who are different from them, to banish entire cultures from crossing their borders in the name of *security*? All of that makes it a Hel of a lot easier for Nott to prey on their fears. And ultimately, to destroy them."

"Wow," I whispered. "You think she's behind all of that?"

"I know she is," Tore confirmed. "She's got a bug in the ear of the administration of nearly every major power in Midgard. Some leaders are strong enough to resist her messaging, but some . . ." Tore just shrugged.

"So, what can we do?" I asked.

"We keep fighting. We fuse the five pieces of Gud Morder that we have; then we hunt for the final three. We take out Nott and any other entities we discover to be aligned with her agenda. We ensure Midgard retains its free will, and we hope its citizens make good choices with that will. Asgard has fought against the darkness for thousands of years. And we'll continue to do so for thousands more."

"What about the traitor?" The rising tide of anxiety crept up my centers. "Did Hjalmar or Vidar say anything else about the security breach in Asgard?"

Tore frowned. "I haven't had a chance to talk to them. But I asked Mack to open up an investigation of our own. He looked into some leads while you were in the healing unit."

"Anything I should know about?" I asked.

Tore gave my armor one final tug and stepped back. He placed his hands behind him on the island, so his triceps popped as he leaned backward. *Mmm, Tore's arms.* Their perfection made the anxiety tide ebb.

"Stay away from my father," Tore cautioned.

"You think your dad's the traitor?" My mouth fell open. "No way. He's sworn to protect Asgard, right?"

"No, I don't think my dad's the traitor," Tore said. "But I think someone in his circle could be. He and the Alfödr are the only gods who would have been privy to our locations on the occasions we were ambushed."

"What do you mean?" I asked.

"I didn't know this before, but Heimdall is obligated to report our Bifrost excursions to the Alfödr and Revenge, since they oversee our mission. Whenever we left Midgard, those two parties would have received a direct communication from Heimdall confirming the occupants and landing coordinates of the Bifrost. Which means that anyone with access to those reports could have known where we landed, tipped off Nott, and contributed to an ambush. We've been attacked so many times, there's no way Nott doesn't have somebody helping her track us. I mean, nobody's *that* unlucky."

"True." I paused. "Wait. Your dad is overseeing our mission?"

Tore groaned. "Technically yes. I have to type up a report once a week for him to deliver to the Alfödr. Because Nott harmed your mother and stole Gud Morder, this falls within his jurisdiction. He wants to see that revenge is served."

Oh, I was going to serve revenge, all right. With Nott's head on a Gud Morder stick.

"And you don't suspect anybody in the Alfödr's team because . . ."

"His security is too tight." Tore crossed his arms. Now his biceps popped against his t-shirt. "Nobody makes it into his camp without undergoing a vetting procedure you don't even want to imagine. And they're subjected to regular probes that would . . ." Tore shuddered. "It's highly unlikely the traitor comes from the Alfödr's team."

"Fair enough. Does Mack have a suspect?" I asked.

"Not yet. But he will."

"Good." I shivered. "We still have three pieces to find. It'd be great if we could just pick them up without being attacked by killer dragons, or psychopathic night elves, or whatever crazy Nott has access to that day."

"It would be nice," Tore agreed. "But even if we do identify the traitor, I wouldn't hold my breath for an easy extraction. If Nott knows where those final three pieces are hidden, she's going to have security on them like you wouldn't believe."

"Well then." I stepped closer to Tore and slid my arms around his waist. Just touching him simultaneously calmed my energy and spiked my heartrate. "Let's just hope she doesn't know where they are."

"Easy as that, huh?" He placed his hands possessively atop my butt. *Oh, mother of all yums.*

I lifted my chin and stood on my tiptoes. "You know what they say. Intention is nine-tenths of the law."

"I believe that's *possession* is nine-tenths of the law." Tore bent down low, so his lips brushed against mine when he spoke. "But yeah, let's intend the Hel out of this thing. What do we have to lose?"

Since the answer to that question was our lives, the lives of all mankind, and the existence of the planet as we knew it, I didn't bother to respond. Instead, I reached one hand up to cradle the back of Tore's head, wrapped my fingers through his hair and pulled him closer. I claimed his mouth in an intense kiss that had his hands snaking up the back of my shirt to rake his fingers down my back. Heat pooled in my belly as Tore palmed my butt. *Holy mother.* If we didn't get ourselves to Bora Bora very soon, I might actually die.

"Come on, guys. We have a weapon to fuse," Bodie chided from over Tore's shoulder. I looked up to find him standing in the kitchen doorway, clutching a thick, velvet bag. Inside, I presumed, were the two assembled—and three non-assembled—pieces of Gud Morder. I still wasn't clear on the rules of my weapon—Nott had said I was the only one who could touch the pieces while they were hidden, but it looked like once I'd freed them, all bets were off. Either that, or Greta had enchanted the velvet so the pieces could be transported.

"What's the deal with the pieces?" I asked. "Nott said I was the only one who could touch them, but obviously, that's not true."

"It's partly true," Tore explained. "The failsafe the gods placed on the weapon meant that once the pieces were separated, only the rightful wielder of Gud Morder—that's you—would be able to retrieve them. But once retrieved, anyone sworn to protect the light realms has the power to access them. We sent the Muspelheim piece back with Mack, while you were in the healing unit."

"Huh." I mulled that over.

"Gud Morder's creators knew there was a chance you might run into trouble someday, so they needed a failsafe that would allow those loyal to you to assist you in your mission. But be assured, *you* are Gud Morder's commander. The weapon is bonded only to you. While the rest of us may carry it, you're the only one who can control it. And if by some horrible mistake it falls into Nott's hands, you'll be able to call it back to you using the crystals in your armor. Remember?"

"Right," I said slowly. I was going to need all of this explained to me again later. Possibly multiple times.

"If you guys are done making out already, we've got a weapon to heal." Bodie pointed toward the back door.

"Right." With a groan, Tore released me from his embrace. He twined his fingers through mine and led me to the back door. Once he'd ushered Bodie and the weapon pieces through, he turned and leaned down low to whisper in my ear. "You. Me. Bora Bora. Soon."

"Clothing optional," I whispered back.

And with grins that were *totally* inappropriate given the direness of our situation, we followed Bodie through the snow and into the complex.

****

Inside the complex, Greta had laid out a special blanket and lit a candle. The flame glistened across the cold metal of Gud Morder. I was thankful to be here, alive, surrounded by friends and healing my weapon. Fusing the pieces meant we were another step closer to waking my mom and healing Midgard. And to Bora Bora.

Greta looked up at me, her moss-colored eyes narrowed in a serious gaze.

"As you know, Gud Morder continues to strengthen as we fuse more pieces. I'm afraid that this time I can't help you—the weapon's power might overtake me."

"Okay," I squeaked, trying to sound like Greta's words didn't worry me one bit.

Yeah, right.

Greta instructed me to hold one of the broken pieces in one hand and the fused piece in the other. My armor vibrated the second I did what she said. The pulse rocking my shoulder was so strong, my entire arm trembled.

Greta nodded in approval. "Good, you won't need the crystal wands this time. There are enough bound pieces that I think you'll be able to manually merge the new ones. Give it a try."

With deep breath, I shoved the broken piece into the fused piece. A shock wave blew outward, cutting Greta off mid-sentence and sending her falling on her butt. Gud Morder glowed but not with the light blue glow I'd seen before. This glow flared so brightly with the deep blue of the Liv that I had to look away.

"Don't let go!" Greta exhaled from her place on the floor.

Don't worry, not an option right now. A fierce groan escaped my lips, and Killer looked up from his chewed-tree-branch-strewn corner to let out a series of barks.

"Allie?" Tore asked.

I just shook my head. My hands trembled as the weapon grew hot. My fingers flexed, wanting to escape the sweltering heat of the metal on my skin. But I locked them in place. My demigod healing would be tackling blisters, and possibly first degree burns, by the time this was over.

"How you doing, Allie?" Tore leaned forward, as if he was ready to jump in at any moment.

Every cell in my body seemed to be moving, rearranging, bubbling. Even if I'd been able to talk, I couldn't have articulated the weirdness of these feelings. The vibrations mingled with the heat and the light, until finally, a loud pop filled the complex. The sensations died down after that, diminishing to little more than a mild buzz.

"Allie?" Tore's voice was more urgent.

"I'm fine," I said. Tore stumbled backward when I looked at him. "What?"

Mack clasped his hands in prayer. "Your eyes. They're glowing with the Liv."

My poor eyes. First the dragon streak, and now this?

Greta rose to stand. "Allie's coming into her full power."

I looked at her nervously. "Full power? Like more powerful than a blue, glowy whip and a telepathic dragon?"

"You're going to need a lot of power to defeat Nott," Greta reminded me.

With a sigh, I looked down at the remaining two pieces of the weapon. "So, I need to do that two more times?"

Greta nodded.

"But you can take a break. Maybe wait for the freaky, glowing eyes to fade?" Bodie chimed in.

I cut him a glare, and he blanched. "Freaky, glowing eyes? Thanks."

He shrugged. "Sorry."

Johann made a cross with his fingers, "Seriously, Allie, I feel like I'm watching a horror movie."

I glowered. "Ha. Ha. Better be nice, or I'm going to stand all glowy eyes over your bed at night while you're sleeping."

Johann swallowed hard. "Seriously. Don't do that."

Bodie and Mack busted up laughing, covering their faces in a poor attempt to conceal their amusement.

Greta put her hand on my shoulder. "Ignore them. Let's finish this, and then I think you should lie down."

That was probably a good idea.

With slightly more hesitation, I picked up the next piece. It went a bit easier than the previous one, maybe because my body was already attuned to the intensity of the heat and the vibration and the cellular restructuring. By the time I fused the tip, an especially strange process because 'attaching' it left a foot-long, invisible energy string in the sword, poor Johann looked like he was about to wet his pants. I could hardly blame him—when I finished bonding the weapon, the entire complex glowed with brilliant blue light. And I was more than happy to lay Gud Morder on the cloth and blow out the candle.

"Now we relax. Right?" I asked the group.

"Right. I'm so proud of you, Allie." Tore stepped closer and was about to sweep me into his arms when the ground shook. It took me a second to realize what was going on—at first I thought it was a leftover vibration from the Liv.

But when Johann shouted, "Earthquake!" everything fell into place.

Literally.

"Take cover," Tore yelled.

Tore threw me to the ground with the force of a speeding train, while Bodie grabbed Greta and hauled her over to the foam practice mats. He lifted one over their heads as he pulled Greta close to his side. I crawled over to wrap my fingers around Gud Morder, nearly falling on the freshly-fused blades as I wobbled back toward Tore. The earth shook harder and glass shattered from the windows above, sending shards of tumbling glass onto the ground. Killer's whines grew louder as he scooted over to Tore. The complex was open by design—we didn't have any tables to hide beneath, so we all stayed low to the ground as we waited for the quake to pass.

"Should we go outside?" I shouted to Tore. I could barely hear myself over the creaking of wood and the groaning of trees.

"No. Get beneath the mats. They'll protect us from the glass." Tore pointed to the stack of mats where Bodie and Greta were huddled together. I crawled on freshly-cut arms to take shelter beneath the thin layer of foam. Tore followed unsteadily, and we were quickly joined by Mack, Killer, and Johann. We held the mats over our heads, the foam providing enough protection to keep our backs from being cut by the bits of glass and debris that rained down. I prayed that the roof wouldn't give way and crush us.

"How long will it last?" I shouted. The earthquake must have been going on for a full minute already.

Tore's eyes widened as a large crack sounded from above. "I have no idea," he shouted back.

Beside us, Mack sat in calm meditation beneath his mat. "Don't worry, the complex is built to withstand this."

I really hoped he was right.

The shaking stopped as suddenly as it had begun. Just like that, the world went eerily quiet.

"What was that?" I was in shock. I'd never experienced an earthquake before, but something told me this hadn't been the run-of-the-mill plate shift. This had to be something more.

"That," Tore gritted through clenched teeth, "was Nott."

Oh. No. She. Didn't.

"How do you know?" I sat beneath my mat, dumbfounded.

"It just adds up." Tore clenched his fists. "The bird, the traitor, all of it."

I struggled to keep up. "What bird?"

He seemed too angry to speak, so Greta did it for him. She emerged from beneath her mat with bits of glass in her hair.

"Do you remember when the Alfödr's raven was shot down inside our shield? It was the night I taught you to use the light whip," she reminded me.

"Of course. But what about him?" I asked.

"We thought a Midgardian tranquilizer took Huginn down. But I ran some tests back at the healing unit. It turns out the dart didn't contain a Midgardian tranquilizer at all. It held a similar serum, one made from a rare flower that only grows on Svartalfheim—the realm Nott adopted when she was banished from Asgard."

My jaw dropped. "She knew we were here?"

Tore seemed to have found his voice. "More likely, one of her scouts was trailing Huginn through the realms, hoping to find us. But I guess now she finally knows where we are. Come on, we need to get outside; this structure won't be stable for long."

I let Tore help me stand, and the six of us, plus Killer, made our way across the debris. The barn door hung on its hinges, but we pushed it aside and stepped out into the snow. When I glanced over my shoulder at the safe house, my knees gave out, and I stumbled forward. Our home was completely ruined. The roof had caved in, and the house appeared to have slid several feet off its foundation. The huge wrap-around porch lay in pieces on the ground. Everything was . . . destroyed.

"The safe house was built in the sixties, but the complex was just put in." Mack shook his head. "We were lucky to be where we were."

Greta was the first to snap out of her shock. "Come on, we should go and see if the neighboring properties need help. Mack, turn off the water and the gas. Bodie, can you see if the garage survived? If you guys still have the quad in there, it sure would come in handy."

Greta was so calm—she must have been used to dealing with crises in her work at the healing unit. I, however, wanted to rock in a dark corner and cry.

"It should be fine. We added the garage a few years ago, and it's reinforced with roughly the same specs as the complex." Bodie took off toward the house, leaving the rest of us to stare at the destruction. My God, the trees. Dozens of amazing, majestic, beautiful redwoods had been uprooted. They lay fallen on the ground, framed by a sea of dead birds. Our forest looked like a war zone. It was yet another casualty in Nott's Night War.

My grip tightened around Gud Morder. How dare she? How could she wreak this level of destruction on such a pristine, innocent place? How could—

"Allie!" Greta's frustrated tone brought me back to the present. She must have been saying my name for a while.

"Sorry. What did you say?"

Greta met my eyes. "There will be injured humans. Can you help me heal them? Bodie can erase their memory of the healing."

Bodie could what? I shook myself. "Yes," I said. Because I needed something to do, or I would fall apart in a puddle of tears. Or possibly fury.

Tore looked at Johann. "We need to find another safe house. Stat."

An engine gunned, and I raised Gud Morder, ready to attack with my partially-constructed weapon. But the sound was just Bodie riding the four-wheeler away from the remains of the house. He came to a stop in front of us and turned his attention to his phone. After a moment, he shook his head.

"What is it?" I asked.

He looked like he couldn't find the words. "There was an eight-point-zero in one country on every continent. This wasn't targeted solely at us—Nott affected the entire world."

"We have to destroy her," I urged. Killer barked his agreement.

One way or another, the night goddess was going down. The question was, how many lives would she ruin before we finally managed to kill her?

CHAPTER FIFTEEN

OVER THE NEXT FEW hours, we worked tirelessly to aid the residents of the two nearby properties. We'd never met the McNealys or the Petersons, having magically shielded our top-secret Asgardian safe house and all. But they accepted our story of being local college kids who just wanted to help. The Petersons lived in a newer build, and while they were heartbroken over losing generations of family heirlooms, not to mention the playhouse they'd hand-built for their now-grown children, they were grateful to have escaped the earthquake without any injuries of their own. The McNealys hadn't fared as well— luckily, Mrs. McNealy had been outside playing with her kids when the quake hit. But her husband had been trapped under debris and was extremely thankful when Tore and Bodie freed him.

I worked on autopilot to heal the fracture in Mr. McNealy's leg. When I was done, Bodie and Greta worked on his memory, and I went outside to soak in the sight of the McNealy children playing together. Their laughter was the lone spark of happiness in my day.

When I'd committed the image of the joyful children to memory, I walked toward the end of the long driveway. Tore and Johann were huddled near the quad, deep in conversation.

"It's the only option, and you know it," Johann pressed.

As I got closer, they schooled their expressions into complete neutrality.

"Oh, stop. I heard you. What's wrong?" I asked.

Tore sighed. "You've been through enough."

"We all have. Look at this place!" I threw my arms up.

"True." Tore accepted that with a nod. "We need to move to a new safe house. Trondheim's our only option. We will be stronger there, surrounded by our ancestors, but . . ."

Norway? The boys wanted me to move to Norway? "But?" I pressed.

"But, I spent time there as a child. We all did— even Nott. It's our Midgardian motherland, and she'll be expecting us to show up there. We'll have to take extreme precautions, use only the strongest shields. If we go there, I'll ask the Alfödr to fit us with the best security measures Asgard can offer."

I couldn't speak. The shock of the day had finally settled in. Instead of refusing to move halfway across the world or arguing that we should just give up on poor Earth and spend whatever days we had left on Asgard, I simply nodded.

Tore looked surprised at my immediate approval. "Okay," he said. He turned to Johann with a determined grimace. "Make whatever calls you have to in order to get us set up. We're moving to Trondheim."

"On it." Johann jumped on his phone.

A silent understanding passed between Tore and me, and we wasted no time getting back into action. We finished our work with the McNealys, packed up what we were able to salvage from the house, and delivered both the four-wheeler and the contents of our freezer and pantry to our neighbors. The roads were completely ruined, and even if they made it to the local grocery store, it would be a while before the shelves could be restocked. No delivery trucks were getting anywhere near town for a very long time. Nott had made sure her earthquake cut the humans off from *everything*.

Four hours after the quake, we lifted off the back lawn of the safe house in a private helicopter Tore had procured from God knows where, since the local airports were shut down. Mack's eyes misted as we flew over the remains of the safe house and into the open sky. "It was a beautiful home," he whispered.

Poor, sweet Mack. The water, broken plaster, and wood chips had sent his inner neat freak into a state of shock. Killer rested his head atop Mack's knee as if he sensed the light elf's sorrow.

"It was, but our next home will be, too," I offered. I had no idea if that was true. For all I knew, we were on our way to live out our final days in a yurt colony.

"It's going to be okay, Mack." Greta reached over to touch Mack's knee. He gave her a tight smile.

"Thanks."

We stared silently out the windows for a long time. As we flew over a snow-capped mountain range, a thought flashed across my mind.

"Hey, how do we know Trondheim survived Nott's attack? Wouldn't she level that place if she knew it was important to you guys?"

Bodie shook his head. "Nott wishes she could bring down Trondheim. It's protected. You'll see when we get there."

Bodie's cryptic comment made zero sense, but I was too exhausted to push the issue.

Tore took my hand in his. He gently stroked my palm with his thumb. "The three primary Norns live at the base of Yggdrasil, the world tree that connects the nine realms. But the Norns who serve beneath Urd, Verdandi, and Skuld have a special affinity for Norway, and specifically for Trondheim. They vacation there, spend years at a time living and working among the mortals. They could sell you your coffee or farm your fruit, and you wouldn't know. They have a deep love for the land there—the Norns would never let Trondheim fall."

I blinked at my boyfriend. "The Norns as in, like, the fates? The ones who prophesized that I would kill Nott?"

Tore nodded in reverence. "The very same."

Whoa.

Greta met my eyes with a small smile. "It's okay," she mouthed.

Was it? I scanned the faces of my friends. Every one of them looked broken. The earthquake had shaken more than the ground—it had shaken our morale. And I had no idea how we were going to get it back.

We rode out the next hour in silence. When we reached an airport that hadn't been affected by the quake, we exited the helicopter and boarded a private jet. Leather recliners awaited inside, and I crashed into the first one I came to. Tore took the seat directly across from me, looking every bit as exhausted as I felt. I was vaguely aware of Killer laying atop my feet. I liked Tore's dog, but I also missed Scarlet. I knew the boys had sent her back to Nidavellir to be with Milkir, and I hoped she'd be happy until I was able to visit her again. I closed my eyes and pictured her crimson scales and twinkling eyes.

'Miss you, girl.' I pressed the thought into the universe. And as I drifted off to sleep, I could have sworn I heard Scarlet's voice inside my head, letting me know she missed me, too.

****

Dragons and birthday cakes danced through my head for what seemed like just minutes, but when I peeled my eyelids open again, the rest of our party was awake, alert, and either zipping up their bags or stuffing them beneath their leather seats. The ground approached outside my window, and my team was preparing to disembark. How long had I been out?

"Hey, Allie." Tore reached over to stroke my cheek. "We're getting ready to land."

"Are we in Trondheim?" I must have slept the entire way.

He nodded. "I asked the pilot to put us down in a field near a farm that my mother used to bring me to. I loved that place—they grew the sweetest lingonberries I've ever tasted."

Johann piped up from behind me. "We can hike to the safe house from there. The Alfödr is having it swept for threats, but the shields should be set by the time we arrive."

Killer nuzzled my knees, and I scratched his ears as the plane landed. I'd just flown in a private jet to Norway. *Norway!* No big deal. *Snort.* We touched down in a smooth landing, and a few moments later, the pilot and co-pilot stepped out of the cockpit to open the door for us.

"Have a safe trip." They waved as we grabbed our bags and exited the plane.

"Thanks," I murmured.

There was indeed a little airstrip on the dirt. From what little I knew of farming, I surmised the field was mostly used by crop dusters. The landing strip certainly wasn't sturdy enough to support a commercial jet, but it was plenty big to support our little ten-seater. I just hoped we hadn't disturbed what appeared to be a quiet farming community with our impromptu travel plans.

"Well?" Tore came up from behind me. "What do you think?"

I turned a complete circle and took it all in. Wide open fields with rows of flowers and greens waved in the light breeze. Colorful farmhouses dotted the horizon, and the sky was a brilliant blue that was a near-perfect match to Tore's eyes.

"I think it's beautiful," I said honestly.

"Glad you like it." Tore placed a hand on my lower back and gently guided me forward. "Pilot wants to take off," he offered by way of explanation. The minute we cleared the runway, the plane's engines surged to life, and in moments the airplane had soared out of view.

"Guess we live here now," I deduced.

"That we do." Mack bowed in his Namaste pose. "Allie Rydell, *velkommen til Norge.*"

"Yeah," Bodie chimed in. "Welcome. First time in Scandinavia, huh?"

"Yes," I answered honestly. "First time overseas, actually. Though I have done a fair amount of inter-realm travel in recent weeks."

Bodie laughed. The entire mood of our crew had lifted; everyone was smiles, and laughter, and *velkommen*-s. I couldn't help but smile, too. Trondheim had some seriously happy juju. I understood what Bodie had meant about it being a special place. The whole town lit up with an energy that was similar to the Liv's—strong and pure and life-affirming. I took in the rows of crops, the people picking the harvest, and the children running in a nearby field. I was just about to tell Tore how much I adored our new home, when a garbled cry escaped his throat. I put my hands on his chest in concern.

"Tore?" I asked.

But he gently pried my hands away and took off at a sprint. He tore through the crops, his feet pounding heads of leafy, green lettuce as he crashed through the field shouting the last word I expected to hear. "Mom!"

"What?" Bodie followed Tore with his gaze. He looked every bit as confused as I felt.

Unsure of what else to do, we dropped our bags and ran after Tore. When we caught up to him, he stood, dumbfounded, in front of a blonde-haired farmer. She wore dirt-covered pants and an oversized hat. But on closer inspection, she looked exactly like the woman in the picture he'd shown me back in my room in Canada. But that was impossible. Tore's mom was dead.

Wasn't she?

"Mom!" Tore tried to hug the woman, but she shrank back.

"I'm sorry, do I know you?" Her hands were crusted with dirt, and her face showed signs of long days in the sun. But she was definitely the woman from the picture.

So, why didn't she recognize her son? And how the hell was she alive?

Tore looked like he had been punched. His mouth opened and closed, but no words came out. Finally, he croaked, "Bodie?"

Bodie just stood there, gaping. Mack and Johann wore twin expressions of confusion, and even Greta seemed to be at a loss. I tuned into the woman's energy and gently probed to see if I could figure out what was going on. The woman's lower five centers seemed fairly normal—radiant green mixed with the same shade of Liv-blue I'd seen in Tore when he'd dropped his shield. But the woman's head was another story entirely. The centers were warped, their coloring faded. Everything was out of focus, as if the centers had somehow been wiped clean. This woman had sustained a high level of brain damage, but whether it was energetic or physical, I couldn't tell.

"Her brain . . ." I didn't know what to say. "Bodie? Can you remind her?"

Bodie took a deep breath and introduced himself, shaking the woman's hand with barely-contained emotion. He told her that there was a bug on her hat, and she allowed him to reach up to touch her head. Some of the darkness in her sixth center receded with whatever Bodie was doing with his gift, but the haze didn't clear. My heart sank. Whatever he'd done hadn't fixed her.

Bodie pulled his hand back. "Her memories are gone. I can't fix this. I'm so sorry, Tore."

Tore turned to look at me, a helpless expression in his endless blue eyes. I took his hand in mine and squeezed, lending all the support I could. The guys and Greta moved closer to Tore, stepping forward to place supportive hands on his arms and back. Then each of us turned our attention to the impossible reality smiling blankly at us from the middle of a Norwegian lettuce field.

Tore's mother was alive. And she had no idea who she really was.

See what happens next for Allie and her protectors, in

NIGHT WAR SAGA: REDEEMER

Hunt down the weapon pieces, destroy the night goddess, protect Midgard (Earth). That was always the mission . . .

When an unexpected sacrifice turns Allie's world on its head, she discovers her true function within the Asgardian world. Her new purpose has much higher stakes—and significantly bigger dangers—than she ever could have imagined. And as the Goddess of Night unleashes an unparalleled wave of fury across the realms, Allie's dream of a peaceful future with her favorite protector all but disappears. Nott's determined to control Midgard. But Allie has more to fight for than ever before, and she's determined to end the Night War . . . no matter what it costs her.

Mange Takk!

S.T.: *Takk* to Leia, for dreaming up another Asgardian tale with me. I can't wait to see what the crew gets up to in Redeemer. *Mange takk* to the readers who embraced this Norse crew with open hearts and the teams who championed this series from the beginning. Leia and I wouldn't get to dream in Allie's world without your support, and we are beyond grateful you share your reading time with us. *Takk* to our designer Alerim, our editor Eden Plantz, our proofreader Tricia Harden, our brilliant beta readers, and to Stacey Nash for *all the things*. *Jeg elsker deg* to my gorgeous husband and our biggest little blessings from God—I love you to the moon and back. *Takk* to everyone who is a Defender of Midgard—thank you for preserving this amazing realm for future generations. And, as always, *mange takk* to MorMorMa, the Force, the trees, Peet's Coffee, and the makers of Traditional Medicinals Spearmint Tea and McVitie's Caramel Digestives. Because, reasons.

Leia: I have to thank S.T. for embarking on this co-author journey with me! We have created something amazing. Thank you to my release team and Matefinder pack for being so supportive and keeping me smiling. I write these books for you. For all of my readers, I am so grateful. Thank you, Alerim, for the beautiful cover, and Eden Plantz, for the edits. To my supportive family and to anyone I forgot: Thank you!

Also by S.T. Bende

Meet the God of War and his Norse crew in
THE ÆRE SAGA.
THE ÆRE SAGA: PERFEKT ORDER
THE ÆRE SAGA: PERFEKT CONTROL
THE ÆRE SAGA: PERFEKT BALANCE

Meet the God of Winter and his Norse crew in
THE ELSKER SAGA.
THE ELSKER SAGA: TUR (a novella)
THE ELSKER SAGA: ELSKER
THE ELSKER SAGA: ENDRE
THE ELSKER SAGA: TRO
THE ELSKER SAGA: COMPLETE BOXED SET

See the crews together in the bonus
Ære/Elsker crossover novella . . .
THE ASGARDIANS

Stay in touch with S.T. at www.stbende.com.

And get a FREE copy of TUR and stay up to date on
the latest news from S.T. Bende by signing up for
her newsletter at
http://smarturl.it/BendeNewsletter

THE ÆRE SAGA: PERFEKT ORDER

All's fair when you're in love with War. Mia Ahlström just discovered her new boyfriend is the Norse God of War. Choosing Tyr may be the biggest distraction—or the greatest adventure—she's ever had.

Also by Leia Stone

MATEFINDER TRILOGY (Optioned for film)
Matefinder: Book 1
Devi: Book 2
Balance: Book 3

HIVE TRILOGY (USA Today Bestselling)
Ash: Book 1
Anarchy: Book 2
Annihilate: Book 3

NYC MECCA SERIES
Queen Heir: Book 1
Queen Alpha: Book 2
Queen Fae: Book 3

MATEFINDER NEXT GENERATION
Keeper: Book 1

Water Blessed

Stay in touch with Leia:
www.amazon.com/author/leiastone
Facebook: www.facebook.com/leia.stone/